THE ARABIAN NIGHTS

Long ago, in a certain city, there lived two brothers.
Kassim, the elder, married a rich, disagreable wife, but
Ali Baba, the younger brother who was a poor
woodcutter, married a girl with no money but a kind
heart.

One day Ali Baba was cutting wood in a lonely part of
the forest when he heard the sound of galloping horses.
He quickly hid his donkeys and climbed up into a tree.
Not a moment too soon! The noise of the galloping
grew louder and then a band of wicked looking
horsemen—each heavily armed with daggers and
scimitars—swept into sight.

Ali Baba counted thirty of them and then, nine more,
and last he saw their gigantic captain. At a signal from
him they all dismounted, tied up their horses, and each
began to unload his heavy saddlebags. One by one
they took these saddlebags to the foot of the great rock
and, when they had them all piled up ready, the
robber chief, standing in front of a part of a rock that
was as steep as a wall, called out in a loud voice,
'*Open Sesame!*'

With a noise like thunder the rock began to gape.

So begins the story of **ALI BABA AND THE FORTY
THIEVES**—just one of the many tales told by Queen
Shahrazad to be found within this book.

Other books by AMABEL WILLIAMS-ELLIS

THE ARABIAN NIGHTS VOLUME II:
ALADDIN AND OTHER STORIES
FROM THE THOUSAND AND ONE NIGHTS

and published by CAROUSEL BOOKS

The Arabian Nights:

Ali Baba and the Forty Thieves and other stories from The Thousand and One Nights

Stories retold by
Amabel Williams-Ellis

Illustrated by Pauline Diana Baynes

CAROUSEL EDITOR: ANNE WOOD

CAROUSEL BOOKS
A DIVISION OF TRANSWORLD PUBLISHERS LTD
A NATIONAL GENERAL COMPANY

THE ARABIAN NIGHTS: ALI BABA AND THE FORTY
THIEVES AND OTHER STORIES FROM THE
THOUSAND AND ONE NIGHTS

A CAROUSEL BOOK 0 552 52036 5

Originally published in Great Britain in one volume
by Blackie & Son Limited under the title *The Arabian Nights*

PRINTING HISTORY

Blackie edition published 1957
Blackie edition seventh imprint 1970
Carousel edition volume one published 1973

Copyright © 1957 by Blackie & Son, Limited, and
Amabel Williams-Ellis

This book is set in Baskerville 12/13 pt.

Carousel Books are published by Transworld Publishers, Ltd.,
Cavendish House, 57–59 Uxbridge Road, Ealing, London W5 5SA

Made and printed in Great Britain by
Richard Clay (The Chaucer Press), Ltd., Bungay, Suffolk.

**NOTE: The Australian price appearing on the
back cover is the recommended retail price.**

CONTENTS

To my Mother
HENRIETTA MARY AMY STRACHEY
who taught me to love fairy tales

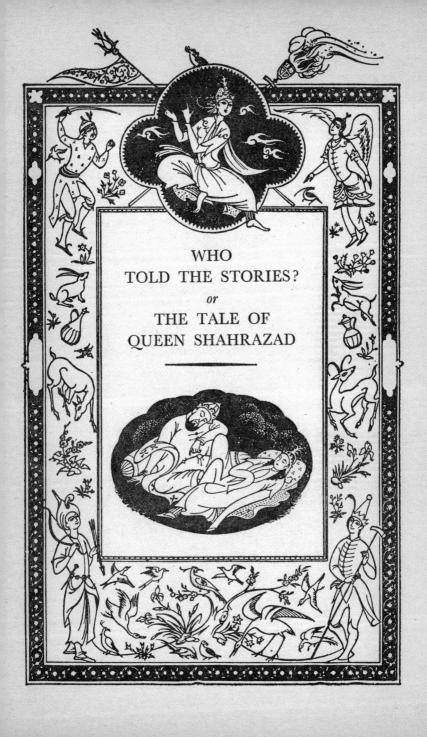

WHO
TOLD THE STORIES?
or
THE TALE OF
QUEEN SHAHRAZAD

In the name of Allah, the Compassionate, the Merciful, Creator of the Universe, Who has raised the Earth without Pillars.

It is said that, long ago, there lived a powerful King who was married to a beautiful Queen. She seemed to love him as dearly as he loved her; but one day he discovered that, in spite of her sweet words and smiles she had been conspiring for many months with his enemies to poison him.

Half-mad with rage, this King not only killed his treacherous Queen—some say with his own hand—but also made a terrible and wicked vow.

He vowed to Allah that however many times he might marry again, he would always have each new wife killed before she had time to plot against him. She would be beheaded—and it would be best if she could be executed on the very morning after the marriage.

For some time the King kept this mad and wicked vow, compelling the Grand Vizier, his Chief Minister, to find beautiful girls for him.

Soon everyone at Court who had a young daughter was careful to send her away to some far country.

Now it happened that the Grand Vizier himself had two daughters, but, thinking that the King would at least not ask him for the life of one of his own children, he did not send them away, but just kept them (as he thought) safely hidden in the women's apartments of his own splendid house, which was not far from the Palace.

Alas, one day, to the unfortunate Vizier's horror, the King, sitting high on his jewelled throne, not only told him that he knew of the existence of these girls, but that he wanted the elder one to be his next Queen.

When the Vizier begged for mercy the King threatened him with immediate death if he did not agree to obey at once.

The unfortunate Vizier bowed to the ground before the angry King, but in his heart he decided that he would send his daughters out of the city that very night, and so give up his own life.

The unhappy man went home, got together his grave clothes, ordered mules and disguises and told his daughter Shahrazad and her younger sister Dunyazad to get ready for instant flight.

But the elder girl, Shahrazad, bowing down before her father, begged him not to risk death for her sake:

'Oh my father,' said she, 'Give me in marriage to this King! For either I shall die, and so save your life, and that of yet another daughter of the Moslems, or else, in spite of all, if Allah wills it, I shall live! If I live I shall save the lives of many other maidens—I shall also save you, my dear father!'

Now her father well knew that this daughter of his—Shahrazad— was no ordinary girl. She was not only beautiful but accomplished and she loved reading stories. She read histories, stories of adventure, and many stories in the form of long poems, so that by the time she was grown up she knew more than a thousand wonderful tales.

But what use, thought her father, would her beauty or cleverness be, once she was at the palace and in the power of the King?

She had to plead hard to persuade him to let her go.

But at last, when it seemed to him that she must have a plan, (try as he would, she would not tell him what it was) her father agreed that she should go. She only wanted one thing, she said, this was that her younger sister, Dunyazad should go with her to the palace.

When, next morning, she had been dressed in her bridal dress, which was made of gold, embroidered with silk; when her hair was twined with jewels; and when over everything was arranged a perfumed veil of the finest gauze, she looked so lovely that the attendants wept to see such a beautiful maiden go into such danger. 'By tomorrow,' they said sadly to each other, 'she may be dead!'

In an outer room of the palace Shahrazad took leave of her sister, and as she did so she whispered to Dunyazad:

'Come to the inner chamber tomorrow before the first light carrying two cups of sherbet cooled with snow. Come in as if you meant to take leave of me. But you must not do so immediately. Instead you must present one of the cups of sherbet to the King and another to me. Then I want you to say to me: "Tell me, dear sister, I beg you, as you have so often done before, some strange story, so that we may better enjoy the cool hour before the sun reddens the sky."'

As they parted, Shahrazad added urgently:

'Do not fail me in this, dear sister, for our lives may depend on it!'

Dunyazad, who was a sensible girl, did exactly as her sister had asked her.

In she came, an hour before sunrise, and, as she handed the cups of sherbet to Shahrazad and to the King, she asked her sister if she would tell her a story, as she used to do at home.

'Willingly, dear sister, if this noble King allows,' answered Shahrazad.

The King nodded, sipping his sherbet, and Shahrazad began to tell a tale which she called 'The Story of the Merchant and the Jinn.'

Now this was a strange tale. It was about a merchant, who, journeying to a foreign country, sat to rest under a tree in a deserted garden, there to eat a piece of bread and a date. When he had eaten, the merchant threw away the date stone.

Now in throwing it away, he ought to have called out 'Destoor' which is to say, 'By your leave', but, as he was alone, he did not say it, but just threw away the little stone.

No sooner had he done so than there appeared before him a horrible Jinn of enormous size, who had a drawn sword in his hand, and who, in a voice of thunder, accused him of just having killed his son by hitting him in the chest with the date stone!

The merchant wept bitterly and begged the Jinn to
spare his life.

'Allah be my witness,' said the unfortunate merchant, 'I meant no harm, it was only a date stone! I am
not ready to die! I have a wife and children that I love,
also I have not paid my debts nor set my affairs in
order!'

But the Jinn only answered that he must die. So at
last the merchant promised that, if the Jinn would
spare his life for a while (so that he could appoint
guardians for his children, and pay his debts) he would

come back on that very same day next year to that very spot. After that the Jinn could do what he liked with him. To this bargain the Jinn at last agreed, and the merchant went sadly home, set his affairs in order, told his wife and children what had happened, and, taking his grave clothes under his arm, said farewell to

his weeping household, travelled sorrowfully back to the deserted garden, and, punctual to the very day, kept his promise to the Jinn.

But when she had got as far as that in the story Shahrazad broke off, saying with a sigh, that there was no time for more, for the sun had now risen.

'But what happened to this unfortunate merchant?' asked the King.

'Ah!' said Shahrazad. 'The things that happened to him were very strange. Indeed this is nothing compared to the next part of the tale, which I would gladly tell if I had time.'

'By Allah!' said the King, 'I too should like to know whether that evil Jinn did indeed kill the honest merchant.'

'Tomorrow, if the King spares me,' Shahrazad replied, 'I will tell.'

So the King got up, and he went as usual to sit in

judgment on his jewelled throne in the great court of the palace.

Now all that night the unfortunate Grand Vizier had spent mourning in his lonely house—too sad to eat or sleep—and next morning, when he came as usual to prostrate himself before the King where he sat upon his throne, he had brought grave clothes for his daughter. The King said nothing at all about Shahrazad, but, as was his custom, received ambassadors from foreign lands and sat in judgment, and all without telling the unfortunate Vizier one word of what had happened to Shahrazad. Yet, as he had not been given the body of his daughter, the old man went home with a little hope that perhaps she still lived.

In the palace next morning, an hour before the dawn, Shahrazad's younger sister once more brought in cups of sherbet cooled with snow, and, once more, begged her sister to go on with the story of the Merchant and the Jinn.

Shahrazad asked the King's permission and, when it was granted, she went on with the story. She told how, as the merchant sat sadly in the deserted garden, which was the place where he had to meet the Jinn, he was joined by a handsomely-dressed man who led a gazelle

by a golden cord, and then by a second man who led two black hounds on chains of silver. They both sat down to rest and began to ask the merchant why he sat alone in the deserted garden and why he looked so sad. No sooner had he finished telling them what had happened than the Jinn appeared, looking more frightful than ever and with his sword ready in his hand. The two strangers now begged him not to be in such a hurry, and offered to tell the tales of why the wife of the one had been turned into a gazelle and the two brothers of the other had become two black hounds. If the Jinn liked the stories and thought them strange enough, they would make a bargain with him; each would ask as his reward half the life of the merchant!

When he had listened to the stories, the Jinn was so astonished that he was quite ready to agree to spare the Merchant's life and said that he did not regret the bargain.

When she had got as far as this Shahrazad again stopped.

'I perceive,' she said, 'that the sun has nearly risen! I wish, O dear sister, and my Lord the King, that there was time to tell you also the story of the Fisherman and the Brass Bottle, for it is really much better and more wonderful than this tale of the Jinn and the Merchant.'

'By Allah,' answered the King, 'if it is an even better tale I must certainly hear it! You shall begin it at the same hour tomorrow!'

Once more, all happened as before. The King heard half the tale, went out and sat on his throne in his Hall of Judgment, but once more he said no word to the unfortunate Vizier.

However, this time, Shahrazad managed to send word to her father in secret to tell him that she was still alive and had good hopes that her plan was going to succeed.

Now, as was said before, this excellent Shahrazad knew and remembered a thousand tales and she was also, as has been shown, particularly cunning in her way of telling them. Sometimes she would tell a story so that one adventure was tangled in another, so that

the King could not be sure of hearing what happened in one story unless he first listened to several other shorter tales. At other times her plan was to tell her stories in such a way that, because of the rising of the sun she had to break off just at some exciting place. She took care, for instance, in the Sindbad story about the 'Valley of Diamonds' to stop at the point when that huge bird, the Roc, had just flown up with Sindbad tied to its leg, and just when Sindbad might (the King would think) at any moment drop off and be dashed to pieces; or when some ship that Sindbad was on seemed to be on the point of sinking.

Hear then some of the tales that Shahrazad thus told.

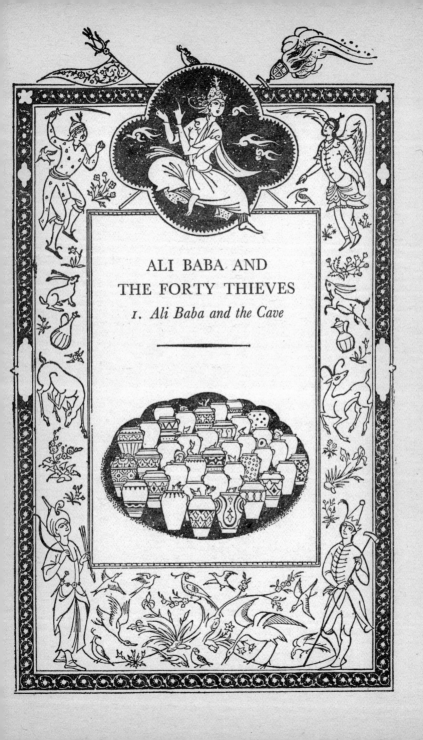

ALI BABA AND
THE FORTY THIEVES
1. Ali Baba and the Cave

Long ago, in a certain city, there lived two brothers. Kassim, the elder, married a rich, disagreeable wife and, with the money she brought him, set up a shop in the market. He was a hard, shrewd, grasping fellow and got very fat, for he made a good living; but he loved himself so dearly that nobody loved him, except his younger brother Ali Baba. Luckily he and his wife had no children. So much for the fat Kassim.

Ali Baba, who earned a poor living as a woodcutter, was very different. He married a good sort of girl with no money but a kind heart. Allah blessed them with a son whom they named Ahmad, but they had no daughter, so they managed to buy a baby girl whom they named Morgiana. The good woodcutter and his wife grew to love this Morgiana and brought her up more like a daughter than a slave, though, indeed, as soon as she was big enough, she was so willing and clever that she did a great deal of work for them. Ali Baba, too, worked hard and, though at first he was so poor that he had to carry his loads of faggots on his back—all the way down from the hills and into the market—the time came when he could afford to buy a donkey and, after a time, two more.

But all this while, when even a small loan of money would have been most welcome, he got no help from his fat, selfish brother. This unbrotherly conduct of Kassim's was all the worse because they lived quite near to each other, so that Kassim and his wife knew perfectly well that, while for instance they were saving up for money to buy another donkey, Ali Baba and his family were often hard put to it to get enough to eat.

One day Ali Baba was cutting wood in a part of the forest where some great rocks marked the foot of the mountains and, while he worked, his three donkeys grazed nearby. His axe rang out loudly among the trees but, pausing for a moment, he heard, in what should have been the silence of that lonely place, another sound. Listening intently, he decided that it was the sound of galloping horses, and he was afraid, for he knew that such a sound, in such a place, boded no good either to him or to his precious donkeys. So he quickly led the beasts off and tied them up where the thick undergrowth hid them and, praying to Allah that none of them would bray and so betray their hiding-place, Ali Baba himself, who had a peaceable nature, climbed up into a tree that stood on a little knoll and gave a good view of the rocks.

Not a moment too soon! The noise of galloping grew louder and then a band of wicked-looking horsemen—each heavily armed with daggers and scimitars—swept into sight. They had dark faces, their great black beards were as coarse as the bristles of pigs and were parted in the middle, in such a way that they looked like the two wings of a carrion-crow.

Ali Baba counted thirty of them and then, nine more, and last he saw their gigantic captain, who looked more evil and ferocious than the rest. At a signal from him they all dismounted, tied up their horses, and each began to unload his heavy saddlebags. One by one they took these saddlebags to the foot of the great rock and, when they had them all piled up ready, the robber chief, standing in front of a part of the rock that was as steep as a wall, called out in a loud voice, '*Open Sesame!*'

With a noise like thunder the rock began to gape.

First there was a crack and then a great split, and when the split was wide enough, each man took up his pair of saddlebags and disappeared inside. When all were in, they were followed by the robber captain. Then Ali Baba heard his voice again, '*Shut Sesame!*' and with the same noise the rock shut upon them.

'Allah grant that they don't, by their sorcery, find me in this tree!' said the terrified Ali Baba to himself, and he fixed anxious eyes on the place where he could see the branches moving as his three precious donkeys stamped at the flies and tugged at their tethers.

As he had no idea what was likely to happen next, or

when the robbers might reappear, he thought it best to stay in his tree. After some time the rock opened again and the robbers all began to file out, this time carrying empty saddlebags. They went straight to their horses, and when all thirty-nine were out and had mounted again, the terrible-looking robber chief came out too and called out, '*Shut Sesame!*'

As soon as the rock had shut again, he, too, mounted, when the whole black-faced, hog-bearded band of ruffians made off at a gallop.

At last, when all the sounds of shouting and horse-hoofs had died away, poor, frightened Ali Baba (thanking Allah that not one of his excellent donkeys had brayed) came down from his tree. His first thought had been for his donkeys, for it was on them that he and his family depended for a living.

But now Ali Baba was overcome with curiosity and, going up to the rock, he examined it carefully. He looked, he felt with his finger, but the rock showed no sign of the split he had seen, indeed there seemed not to be even a crack into which he could have got the point of a needle.

'This place is certainly guarded with a spell,' said he to himself, 'and yet, all I heard them say was the name of a harmless grain—sesame, the grain that my wife buys sometimes to make cakes. I wonder if that is really enough?' And then, in a trembling voice, Ali Baba, turning again to the rock, said softly, '*Open Sesame!*'

To his amazement, the rock at once obeyed and, with a noise like thunder, the great split appeared in its smooth face, and then, once more, the forest was still.

Ali Baba was almost too frightened to look inside, but at last, plucking up his courage, he took a step forward and then he stared with all his eyes. What he had expected to see will never be known, but what is certain is that this was not a dreadful cavern dripping with horror. On the contrary, a dry, level gallery led to a large hall hollowed out of the mountain and cunningly but rather dimly lit by slits contrived in the roof. Ali Baba turned back to the opening and, saying the words which shut the rock (for he feared that if one of the robbers came back he might be seen), he walked boldly on and, in a few steps, found himself in the great cavern.

As his eyes got used to the light he saw that all along the walls, piled up to the roof, were bales of silks, bars of silver and gold, and great chests which were so full of treasure that their contents spilled out on to the floor. Ali Baba could hardly put down a foot without treading or slipping on something precious!

Looking more closely, he saw that some of the gold cups and necklaces and bracelets were of ancient workmanship, and some were new, so that it seemed to him as if this cavern must have been, for hundreds of years, the secret store-place of many generations of robbers.

'Allah be praised!' said Ali Baba. 'For he, who loves to reward the simple, has made me, a poor woodcutter, master of the fruit of terrible crimes. Now, instead of being used by those ruffians, the treasure will be put to the innocent use of a poor family!'

Then Ali Baba began to think once more of his three donkeys, and sat down to consider how much treasure each could carry without being overloaded. He calculated that each must also carry a small load of light faggots so that no one should guess his secret.

He decided to take only coined gold, for, if a poor woodcutter were to try to sell even one of these emeralds and diamonds, or a single cup or bracelet, then who knows what questions and trouble might follow.

So, with modest good sense, Ali Baba only gathered up what it seemed prudent to take—that is, what the robbers would not be likely to miss immediately and what his precious donkeys could easily carry.

Safely Ali Baba once more opened and then closed the rock, safely he brought up his three donkeys, safely he put on to the back of each two small bags of gold nicely hidden with faggots. As they all four walked down the mountain to the city, Ali Baba found himself speaking quite softly and respectfully to his donkeys instead of shouting at them. He told them that they had eyes like dark pools of water—which was true. He called them 'Grey Pearl', 'Silken Ears', and 'Nightingale', instead of 'Obstinate Pig', or 'Stumbler', or 'Daughter of Evil', as he often did (just to make them mind their work). For now he kept remembering that on their humble grey backs they carried enough gold to make a dowry for a princess. So the donkeys— for such is the nature of donkeys—loitered and stopped often to snatch a nice-looking mouthful of grass and, in short, took double their usual time to get back home.

Once safe in his own courtyard, Ali Baba threw

down the faggots and began to take the six small but heavy bags of gold into the house. Now these were bags from the cave and, since they were poor, his wife knew every bag and basket that they had, so she was surprised to see six strange bags, and still more surprised when—to help him—she lifted one of them and found how heavy it was. So she began to ask where they came from.

'These bags are from Allah, good wife! Help me to carry them, and don't torment me with questions!'

'Money!' said the good woman to herself as she heard the clinking, and she supposed that they must be full of copper coins. But six bags even of copper coins seemed to her a great treasure and she began to be frightened, thinking that in some way her good, honest, timid Ali had been up to no good. She even began to beg him to take them away in case they brought bad luck, so, before letting her see what the bags really held, Ali Baba swore her to secrecy, and when, after locking the door, he had poured the flashing gold out on to the floor, she became so frightened that he thought it best to tell her the whole story.

When she heard it, and knew that Ali Baba had been able to bring it all safely and secretly to the house, the poor woman's joy was as great as her terror had been.

2. *Ali Baba and Kassim*

'Help me now, wife!' said Ali Baba when he had finished the tale of the robbers and the treasure-cave. 'We will only keep out a few coins at present and we will dig a trench under the floor of the kitchen and hide the rest of the money.'

'But we must count it first!' said his wife.

Ali Baba laughed. 'Poor, foolish woman!' said he. 'You could never count all that!'

She said she could, he said it would take too long. She began, but after an hour she gave it up.

'But surely, husband, we must at least weigh or measure it? I will do the measuring while you dig under the floor,' she went on. 'Like this we shall know how much our dear son will inherit from us.'

'But we have no measuring bowl or scoop, for we have never been able to buy enough grain or flour at a time to measure anything,' he answered.

'That is true,' said his wife. 'But I will just step round and borrow a measuring scoop from our sister-in-law—Kassim's wife.'

'Be sure you don't say a word about the treasure!' said Ali Baba and his wife, agreeing, promised not to say a word.

Now, though Kassim's wife was so mean that she had never given her nephew Ahmad or the girl Morgiana so much as a sugared chick-pea—the very cheapest kind of sweet—while they were children, she could not very well refuse the loan of a wooden measure for a few minutes. All the same, she was curious to know what sort of grain these poor people had in such quantity that a measure was needed.

'Will you have the small measure or the large one?' she asked.

'The small one, O my mistress, if you please,' answered Ali Baba's wife humbly.

As she was fetching the measure, Kassim's wife thought how interesting it would be just to know what it was wanted for.

'My poor, silly sister-in-law,' said she to herself, 'is sure to put the measure down on the grain, so if I rub a nice, thick bit of suet on to the underside, a little of whatever she is measuring is sure to stick, and then I shall know.'

Sure enough, when Ali Baba's wife got home the first thing she did was to put the borrowed measure down on the top of the pile of gold and, just as Kassim's wife had intended, the suet stuck to what it had been put on, so that a single gold coin remained on the under side and, in this way, Ali Baba's wife—poor creature— was the innocent means of giving away their great secret!

No sooner was the measuring done and the gold buried, than back she ran in a great hurry to her sister-in-law's house and, thanking her for her kindness, gave her back the measure.

Hardly was her back turned when Kassim's wife turned the measure upside down, and what was her amazement to see, sticking to the under side, a shining gold dinar!

Kassim's wife at once felt furiously jealous! The thought that, in her

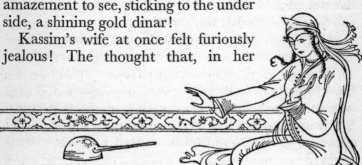

sister-in-law's house, they had so much gold that they measured instead of counting it, was poison to her. However, she just had enough sense not to go shouting to the neighbours about this strange affair. But as soon as her husband came back, she showed him the gold and told him what had happened.

Instead of rejoicing at his kind brother's good luck, Kassim grew yellow with envy and he felt that he could never rest till he not only knew the secret but got some of the gold for himself. So, without waiting a moment, he rushed round to his brother's house.

He found Ali Baba in the kitchen, still with the pick-axe in his hand and, without a word of greeting, and speaking low between clenched teeth, Kassim hissed in Ali Baba's ear:

'O ill-omened brother! How dare you be so secret-ive! Tell me immediately how it is that you—dirty, starved-looking creature that you are—have so much gold that you measure instead of counting it?'

Poor Ali Baba was dumbfounded, and when his horrible brother shook the gold dinar under his nose and threatened to tell the rulers of the town that Ali Baba was a robber and to have his donkeys killed and the whole house pulled about his ears, he at last told Kassim the story, but without telling him the magic words which opened the rock.

'The words! The words that open the cave!' said Kassim, looking furious. 'Don't dare to hide anything!'

'Dear brother,' answered Ali Baba gently, 'we are the children of one father and one mother! I will willingly share the treasure with you, good brother! But don't ask me the words! To prove that I am in earnest you can have half of all that I brought home to-day.'

'No!' answered the black-souled Kassim. 'The

32

words! I must know the words! I want to be able to go there myself! Tell me directly or I will tell everyone that you stole the gold.'

So, though he feared that evil would come of it, Ali Baba was obliged to tell his brother both the way to the rock and the words which opened the treasure-cave.

Now Allah contrives many ways in which to bring the wicked and heartless to destruction, and it was through his own selfish greed that Kassim met with his just reward.

The very next morning, as soon as it was light, Kassim, who had refused Ali Baba's offer to act as guide, stole off secretly with ten mules, each carrying empty sacks. He found his way to the place, tethered the mules, stood before the smooth face of the rock and cried with all his might, '*Open Sesame!*'

When the rock opened he rushed into the cavern and, almost stunned by the sight before him, had hardly breath to give the order that closed the rock again. He saw gleaming silks, cups made of chased gold of exquisite workmanship, jewels fit for the turban of a Sultan, anklets, necklaces, bracelets, earrings, bars of gold, minted money! All this was piled in great heaps right up to the top of the cavern or was littered and scattered about. The sight quite dazzled Kassim and he began to mutter:

'Ten mules? Pooh! Not enough! Twenty mules? Pshaw, only a beginning! Not all the camels of all the merchants that visit our city at the great fair will be enough to carry away all this splendour!'

Talking out loud to himself and rushing from one side of the cavern to the other, fat Kassim began to beat his forehead and scratch his head, trying to think how he would ever be able to contrive to get it all for himself. Soon he began to collect 'just a little' (as he called it to himself) into the sacks that he had brought. But he was so greedy that he was always unpacking a sack in order to put in something still more valuable that had just caught his eye and, being very fat, he was soon quite breathless and exhausted. At last, still thinking how he could get yet more, he began to drag his heavy sacks to the end of the gallery and to pile them up. It was not till he was nearly fainting with his effort and his wild excitement that he decided to go.

And now it was that Allah turned Kassim's shocking greed against him, for, in his excitement, and thinking only of his wild plans to keep all the treasure to himself, he found that, when he needed to speak it, he had forgotten the word! He stood thinking! It was the name of a grain—he knew that much—but which grain?

'*Open Barley!*' he cried. '*Open Millet!*' '*Open Wheat!*' But all in vain: the rock remained shut. He began to be afraid. '*Open Rice!*' '*Open Rye!*' Still it was of no use.

There he stood, speechless now, and growing more and more terrified and confused. At last he heard a noise like thunder and a crack of light began to appear. It was the robbers! They had come back, had seen the mules, had leapt from their horses, had looked everywhere for the mules' owner, and now their chief, pointing his drawn sword at the rock, had spoken the magic words, '*Open Sesame!*'

Kassim, guessing the terrible truth, made a wild rush for freedom as the rock split, only, at the very entrance, to be cut into six pieces by the swords of the furious robbers. The thieves laughed loudly, wiped their swords, tossed the wretched fragments inside, emptied out the sacks of treasure that Kassim had piled up, and then had a look to see if anything else seemed to have gone. But so great was the mass of treasure that they never missed the six small bags of gold that the careful Ali Baba had gathered from here and there.

And now the forty robbers sat in a circle discussing (as well they might) how this greasy citizen, who had not looked the sort of man who ever came to the forest, could have discovered their secret. They got angry, so that, if it seemed that one of them had accidentally betrayed it on a visit to the town, the others were soon quite ready to cut off his head and to leave him to keep company with Kassim.

Unable, talk as they would, to guess how this strange and awkward event had happened, they decided to leave Kassim's body in the gallery, where, said the robber chief, it would be a warning if anyone else, by ill fortune, had also discovered the way to the cave.

Now all that day, Kassim's wife, who alone knew where he had gone, waited in vain for him, and so it was that, when night fell, she went wailing to Ali

Baba's house to beg his help. But it was now pitch dark, so, till morning came, all that Ali Baba and his wife could do was to try to comfort the weeping woman. She, to tell the truth, was quite as much crying and wailing because the treasure might be lost, as for fear of what might have happened to her fat husband.

As for Ali Baba, he was truly troubled about his brother; he had forgotten all Kassim's heartlessness and only remembered how they had played together as boys. So the dawn was scarcely grey in the sky before the good Ali Baba and his three donkeys once more set out for the forest.

First he hunted about for his brother's mules, but the robbers had taken them all, and when he did not see them Ali Baba grew terribly afraid. When, at the threshold of the rock, he saw a stain of blood he shuddered for pity, so that it was in a trembling voice that he cried once more, '*Open Sesame!*'

Alas! What a sight met his eyes! His knees knocked together with terror when he saw the six pieces into which the robbers had hacked Kassim, and cruel and heartless as the dead man had been to him, Ali Baba wept.

'The only thing I can do for you now, my brother, is to give you decent burial, so that your poor ghost shall find rest,' said he to himself and, though he very well understood the danger of what he was doing (for it would mean that the robbers would know that this dead man was not the only one who knew their secret) he found sacks and divided the new load in such a way that it could be put on the backs of his three donkeys and hidden, as the gold had been, with faggots and branches. Then, when all was finished, closing the rock once more, Ali Baba set out sadly on his journey home.

3. Ali Baba and Morgiana

When Ali Baba got back with Kassim's body it so happened that it was not his wife, but their adopted daughter—the slave-girl Morgiana—who came out to meet him and to help him to tie up the donkeys. Ali Baba was glad to see who it was, for he was rather superstitious. Indeed, as he had walked back sadly from the forest with the donkeys, he had been thinking that, perhaps, as it had been through his wife, who had insisted on measuring the gold, that his brother and sister-in-law had discovered their secret, the less the good woman had to do with it all, the better. Though innocent, she might, he thought, bring them all back bad luck again. So he was pleased that it happened to be young Morgiana who helped him to unload, and it was to her that he first told what had happened.

'Morgiana, my pretty one,' he ended, 'we shall need all your wit and cleverness over this! While I go with your adopted mother to break this terrible news to my sister-in-law, you try to think of some way in which we can manage to have a proper funeral. We don't want questions! Somehow the neighbours had better be made to believe that poor Kassim died of a natural illness. But I can't think how it's to be managed!'

With that Ali Baba left her and went into the house and, telling his wife briefly what had happened, they both went off to try to break the news to Kassim's widow in such a way that she would not let out the secret. She really must be persuaded not to do too much loud crying and wailing or else the neighbours would guess that there had been a death.

So young Morgiana sat down and thought, and, being a very clever girl, she soon hit upon an excellent plan. She went off to a certain neighbouring druggist

37

who she knew was a great gossip. When she got to his shop she told him, with a very long face and in a tone as though she were rather frightened, that she had been sent by her master to buy a certain very expensive mixture that was well known to be good against a fever called the Red Evil. 'My master's brother,' she added, 'Kassim the merchant, has suddenly fallen very ill.'

Some hours later she went again.

'Alas,' said she, 'the merchant Kassim grows no better! We fear it may indeed be the Red Evil! His face is yellow, he cannot speak, and seems blind! Allah help him! He hardly moves or breathes! Our only hope is now in your skill, oh most learned druggist!' (Here she seemed ready to burst into tears.) 'Let cost not be thought of! Mix us something so powerful that it will bring my master's poor kinsman back from the very edge of the grave!'

On each walk to this gossiping druggist, as she came and went, Morgiana had taken care to chat with everyone she knew about the sad illness of her master's brother. She told them, moreover, that Kassim had been moved to Ali Baba's house for better care.

The consequence was that, next morning, the neighbours were not surprised to hear piercing cries and lamentations and to be told the news that Kassim the merchant was dead.

Now Kassim, as has been told, had been chopped into six pieces, and it was the custom in that city not to have the dead put into coffins, but to bury them well wrapped in costly shawls.

'We shall have succeeded in nothing, Master, if we cannot manage to make him seem to be all in one piece!' said Morgiana thoughtfully to Ali Baba when he praised her for what she had already done. Ali Baba dolefully agreed, but could think of no way of managing this.

Now there was a poor old cobbler who lived in the district, and what did the excellent Morgiana do but hurry off to him. Slipping one of the gold dinars from the treasure into the old man's hand, she said to him:

'Oh most excellent of cobblers, we have need of your best skill! Also,' and here Morgiana dropped her voice to a whisper, 'we have two more of these gold dinars.'

'If it is anything lawful that you ask me to do, oh excellent and charming one, I will do it!' answered the delighted old cobbler, whose work very seldom brought him one, let alone three, gold pieces.

'It is indeed lawful! In fact it is only a little sewing! But also it is a secret,' replied she. 'So my master has told me that, unless, when you come with me, you will consent to be blindfolded, I am to take the two other gold dinars elsewhere!'

The end of it was that, that night, Morgiana came

to fetch him, and the old cobbler agreed to have his
eyes bandaged, and Morgiana, taking an extra turn or
two for safety, led him round about to a cellar under
Ali Baba's house.

When the old cobbler's first surprise and dismay
were over, he finally did his work very neatly and was
taken back just as he had come.

Thus it came about that Kassim was, once more, all
in one piece, and neatly wrapped in thick shawls and
tidily arranged on a carrying litter. When the Imam
(who was the priest of the nearby mosque) and all the
neighbours assembled for the funeral, no one could
possibly guess that it had been the swords of forty
furious thieves, and not the Red Evil, that had brought
the greedy merchant to his end.

And now, for almost a whole month, peace descen-
ded upon the two households. Ahmad, Ali Baba's son,
who was a pleasant, handsome young man, took over

40

the shop of his dead uncle, and the customers found him so much more agreeable and so much more honest, that the shop prospered more than ever. Ali Baba's wife, who, though perhaps rather a silly, fussy woman, had a very kind heart and a forgiving nature, went to be with her sister-in-law during the time of her widow's mourning. Then, as otherwise Morgiana would now have had all the work of their house on her hands, Ali Baba bought a strong, cheerful young black slave named Abdullah so that, after all that the clever girl had done for them, his dear Morgiana's work should be light.

Morgiana, who truly loved her master and mistress (who were indeed the only father and mother she had ever known), would hardly accept the pretty bracelets, anklets, earrings, and other small presents that the grateful Ali Baba gave her. As for Ali Baba himself, he knew that he had secrets to keep and that he had many inquisitive neighbours, so he was careful not to alter his way of life and so draw attention to himself. So he used very little of the gold under the kitchen floor, but went on, just as before, cutting faggots and selling them. Indeed, except the buying of the young black man, the only change in Ali Baba's way of life, and that of his three donkeys, was that never, never did he turn their grey noses down any path that led anywhere near the rock of the robbers, but cut his faggots as far away from it as he could.

Now the reason why, for nearly a whole month, all had been so peaceful was that the thirty-nine thieves and their captain had ridden off, far out into the desert, to attack a caravan, and it was only after this long journey that they came back to their cave. As soon as the captain had said the magic words and they began to go in with their booty, the very first man saw at once that Kassim's body had disappeared. They were all now much alarmed, for they realized (as Ali Baba had been sure they would) that this meant that some living man knew their secret!

Again they searched the cave, this time more thoroughly. Still they did not miss the small amount of treasure that Ali Baba had taken. Finding that only the dead body had vanished, their surprise was all the greater and they began to quarrel violently with each other, and each man accused another of having, in some way, betrayed the secret.

At last the ferocious robber-captain clapped his hands for silence. Then and there he told them that one of his followers would have to venture, disguised, into the city as a spy and try to find news of a man who had been cut into six pieces.

'Know, before anyone offers himself for this task, that if he fails, or in any way betrays our secret, I shall myself strike off his head with my scimitar!'

In spite of this, one of the thieves at once agreed to go. So, next morning, before it was light, this thief disguised himself carefully as a wandering dervish or holy-man, and went down to the market.

Now when he got there it was still so early that it was scarcely light and most of the shops were still shut, but seeing an old cobbler already in his shop and busy threading a needle, the pretended dervish greeted him politely and remarked what excellent eyesight he must have.

'Yes (thanks be to Allah!) my eyes are good,' answered the cobbler, pleased at the compliment. 'Indeed I can do even better than that! Why, not long ago I even sewed together the six parts of a dead body in a cellar that had less light than we have now.'

The pretended dervish, who had already made out

that he came from far away, said that he was surprised to hear that sewing up the dead was one of the customs of the city.

'Nay, it's no custom here! This was done secretly!' answered the cobbler.

'How very interesting!' answered the pretended dervish. 'I should dearly like to see the house!' And with that he offered the cobbler a piece of money if he would show him.

'How can I show the house to you, O holy man? I was blindfolded and led there by a young slave-girl who took me there and back with many turns and twists!'

The end of it was that, partly by bribery and partly by flattery, the pretended dervish persuaded the old cobbler that he was sure to be clever enough to find the place if he were again blindfolded and allowed to grope his way there.

Alas for Ali Baba and all in his house! The cobbler did, in the end, succeed in leading the disguised robber to the very door.

43

Now the street was a long one with many doors and courtyards, all rather like those of Ali Baba. Determined that there should be no mistake when he  brought along the others, the robber at once pulled a piece of white chalk out of his girdle and marked the door with it and then, having paid and thanked the old cobbler for his trouble, he hurried back to the forest, and there he boasted to the robber-captain about how well and quickly he had done his errand.

Now it so happened that hardly had the cobbler and the pretended dervish left the street, than Morgiana—on her way to the market—came out of the house. Ever since the strange events of nearly a month ago the clever girl had been on the alert and more than ever quick in noticing every little thing, for she felt only too sure that they would not be left in peace for ever. So now, as she left the house, she turned back for a moment, upon which her eye fell on the white chalk mark.

'This did not write itself!' thought Morgiana. 'Some enemy has marked us out for misfortune,' and, slipping back into the house, she got another piece of white chalk, and quickly marked every door and gateway on both sides of the street. Then, well pleased, but still a little uneasy, she went off to do her marketing.

Early next morning, on their captain's orders, the robbers began to come two by two into the city. Not wanting to attract attention, each pair chose a different road. What was their bewilderment, when they met in the street which the first thief had described, to find that not only one, but more than a dozen houses were each marked with the white chalk which was to have been the signal! There was nothing for it but to go back to the forest, where, in his rage, the robber-captain cut off the head of his first unsuccessful spy. The robbers were now more uneasy than ever, for it seemed to them that their enemy must be very much alive, and also exceedingly clever.

There seemed nothing for it but to send another thief to bribe the old cobbler once more. This time, with no difference except that the second robber dressed himself up as a foreign merchant, the same thing was done. This time the pretended merchant made a very small red mark instead of a large white one. But Morgiana was on the look-out now, found the red mark almost as soon as it was made, and, when the robbers crept two by two into the city again, it was to find small red marks on all the doors for half a mile around! When they all got dolefully back to the forest, the second thief met his end.

Then it was that the robber-captain decided that he would go himself. The old cobbler (who was growing quite rich and had decided that sewing corpses paid much better than sewing shoes) told his curious story again to someone who seemed to be a peddler and led this third inquisitive stranger to the house. But the Captain—wiser than his followers—only looked and remembered, and made no mark which could tell Morgiana to be on her guard. As soon as he was back in the forest he quickly ordered his followers—there were now thirty-seven of them—to go disguised to the market and there to buy thirty-eight large oil-jars with wide necks. Each was to be large enough for a man to crouch in. Thirty-seven were to be empty and one was to be full of the very best olive oil.

'I know the house now, and the fate of all who live in it shall be terrible!' added he and, as they got ready, they all sharpened their daggers and scimitars.

Next evening, the unsuspecting Ali Baba, who was tired from his day's work of cutting faggots, was sitting at his door to enjoy the cool air, and, as he sat, he saw a string of laden horses coming up the street. There seemed to be only one man with them, and as he came opposite the house this man greeted him politely.

'O Master,' said the traveller, 'I am an oil-merchant and my horses have come far to-day. I am a stranger here and, as I have fodder for the horses, I venture to ask you, of your kindness, to allow me to tie my horses in your yard and also to give me shelter for the night. If you consent, Allah will bless you for your hospitality.'

Now one of the things that delighted the good Ali Baba was that, now he was no longer so poor, and now that his son Ahmad was an independent shopkeeper, he was usually able to give just such help to strangers. So, answering joyfully, he rose immediately, opened the gates of his yard, and, calling to Morgiana and to the black slave, he told them that they had an honoured guest and that an excellent supper was to be prepared.

He himself bustled about, helping the supposed oil-merchant to set down the heavy oil-jars and tether the horses.

Later, as they ate together at supper, he found the traveller a most interesting companion, for he seemed to have been in many strange lands and had many interesting tales to tell.

At last it grew late and the oil-merchant said that before going to bed he would just like to see that all was well with his horses, so, while Ali Baba and Morgiana went to bring out pillows and mattresses to make him a comfortable bed, the robber-captain—for it was none other—began to talk loudly to his horses in the yard.

'Stop that stamping and fidgeting, White Star!' he would call, and then, when he was near one of the jars, he whispered under his breath:

'When I throw a pebble out of my bedroom window!'

Then aloud he said again, 'Steady, mare! Daughter of a fidgety fiend! If your hoof isn't over your picket rope!' and then, whispering again, 'When I throw a pebble out of my window!' And so he went on, speaking in turn to each robber hidden in each of the thirty-seven jars and telling him the signal at which he was to come out and help in the slaughter.

To the last jar he did not speak, for that one really did contain oil.

When Morgiana had finished helping her master with the bed, and when the supposed oil-merchant was comfortably lying in it, there were still the supper-dishes to wash. As she worked in the kitchen at the washing up, what should happen but that her lamp should run out of oil. She was put out and called the news to the black slave Abdullah, saying how silly she had been to forget to get in enough oil.

'By Allah!' answered Abdullah, laughing. 'How can you say, O my foolish sister, that we are out of oil when, to-night, there are thirty-eight jars of the very best oil just outside in our yard!'

Morgiana hadn't thought of that, but now, taking a ladle, out she went in the moonlight and, taking out the fibre stopper from the first jar she came to, she put in her ladle, which, as luck would have it, hit one of the hidden robbers bang on the head!

'Pebble, Captain?' said a deep, hoarse voice from the jar. 'That was more like a rock! But we are ready!'

48

And with that the jar began to rock as the crouching robber began to raise himself.

Anyone but the excellent Morgiana would now surely have screamed with fright; but, though her mouth was dry and she felt her heart pounding, she managed to whisper, 'Be quiet! Not yet! Not yet!'

As she put back the fibre stopper, she began to realize what the plot must be and, though her knees shook, her lips trembled, and her long black hair almost stood up with fright, she went steadily from one jar to another, tapping on each, and when the deep voice of a robber answered, she repeated again her, 'Not yet! Not yet!'

At last she came to a jar from which there was no answer. Then once more she took out the fibre stopper, put in her ladle, filled it with excellent oil and, returning to the kitchen, at last relighted her lamp.

What was she to do? This had taken some time. All the three men were now asleep—the black slave Abdullah, her master Ali Baba, and the man whom she now knew to be the dreadful captain of the robbers. Then Morgiana thought of a fresh plan.

First she lit a great fire in the kitchen fireplace, and over it she hung the largest cauldron in the house—one which was generally used for boiling clothes. Backwards and forwards went Morgiana with ladle and bucket to the real oil-jar, until she had filled the cauldron. As soon as the oil was boiling she filled their largest bucket with it and, going softly to the first jar, she relentlessly poured into it a great dollop of the

boiling oil, which killed the first robber directly. She
went in this way from jar to jar, till at last her work
was done. Then she went back to the kitchen, put out
the fire and her lamp, and hid herself.

Silently she waited and, at last, she heard that,
upstairs, a window was being opened. The robber-
captain cautiously put out his head and, seeing all the
house in darkness, he supposed that all his intended
victims were safely asleep. Then he took up the pebbles
that he had ready prepared, and began to throw them
one by one at the jars. Though the moon was down and
it was very dark, he could tell by the sound, as they
struck the jars, that his pebbles were reaching their
marks. But there was no answer! No stirring! No rush
of armed men

'The dogs!' he said to himself in a fury. 'They have
all gone to sleep!' Then, creeping downstairs, he went
to the jars. To his horror, each jar felt as hot as an oven,
and, opening each of them in turn, he realized that
they now contained only lifeless corpses! With that the
robber-captain took one leap on to the top of the
courtyard wall, let himself down into the road, ran for
his life down the empty street, and did not stop running till he had reached the safety of his cave.

Morgiana, though she could not see, had heard it all
and, realizing with thankfulness that they were now
safe, waited till the first light of the morning before she
waked her master.

7. Ali Baba and the Invited Guest

Not until it was light did Morgiana wake Ali Baba.
Then, asking him to come down to the courtyard, she
begged him to lift the cover of the first jar.

Ali Baba started back in horror at what he saw, but when Morgiana had told him the whole story of the night, he wept tears of joy.

'O daughter of good fortune! O moon of excellence!' he cried. 'Surely the bread that you have eaten in our house is a little thing compared to this! Henceforward, dear Morgiana, you shall be our eldest child and the head of the house!'

So he and his slave Abdullah spent the rest of the day in digging a great pit in the garden and there, when it was dark, they buried the thirty-seven robbers. It only remained to dispose of the horses, and these they sold one by one, so that the curiosity of the neighbours should not be aroused.

And now, once more, they lived peacefully for a while; but Morgiana was still watchful, for she could not believe that they had heard the last of the terrible captain of the robbers.

It happened that one day Ali Baba's son, Ahmad, who, as was told, had inherited his uncle Kassim's shop, mentioned that a new merchant, who called himself Hussein, had set up a shop near his own. Soon Ahmad began to tell them more about this Hussein. He said he was a venerable man with a long silvery beard and very pious. He said he was a most excellent and hospitable neighbour and was continually doing him some little service or other. At last Ahmad said to his father:

'Five times have I shared the midday meal of this excellent old man. Do you not think, O my Father, that we should return his hospitality?'

Ali Baba agreed at once, so it was arranged that the white-bearded merchant who called himself Hussein should be asked to supper the very next Friday—the day of rest. Hussein, after making a few polite excuses, agreed to come. All day Morgiana, Abdullah the black slave, and a woman (who now did most of the cooking) worked to make a really splendid supper. Hussein was duly welcomed and, while he, Ali Baba, and his son Ahmad ate, Morgiana waited on them.

Now it certainly seemed—as young Ahmad had said —that their venerable visitor had a particularly splendid, long, silvery beard and, as she passed the dishes, Morgiana looked rather closely at this beard. She also noticed that this Hussein had in his girdle a particularly long dagger, and it presently seemed to Morgiana that she had somewhere seen this dagger before. However, she said nothing and, when the last dish had been served, she retired to her own room, leaving the three men to their wine.

What was Ali Baba's surprise, when a few minutes later, he saw Morgiana entering the room again, dressed, not in her usual clothes, but as a dancing-girl.

She seemed to have put on every trinket that he had ever given her! On her forehead were glittering sequins, on her ankles and wrists were clinking silver bracelets and anklets, each set with little rows of tinkling bells, at her neck hung a long string of amber

beads, at her waist was a golden belt, and from the belt hung a jade-hilted dagger. This was an ornament such as dancers often wear so that the dagger, in its long decorated sheath, will swing out in time to nimble dancing feet and clinking anklets.

Young Ahmad gasped at the sight. He had no idea that Morgiana—a girl whom he saw every day busy with the work of the house—could look so lovely! Her eyes, which to-night were darkened with kohl, seemed to glitter with a feverish light, her slender hands and feet were adorned with henna, her long, shining hair swung down to her slim gold-circled waist.

When they could take their eyes off her they saw that

Morgiana was followed by Abdullah the black slave, who beat softly upon a tambourine. First bowing low to the honoured and venerable guest Hussein, Morgiana began to dance as lightly as a happy bird and, as she danced, the rhythm of the tambourine grew louder and stranger for, like most of those of his race, the young Abdullah was a master of rhythm. First Morgiana danced the kerchief dance, then she danced a Persian dance, and all the while the pace of the beat of the tambourine and the clink of her dancing feet grew swifter and swifter. At last signalling to Abdullah, she broke into the slow, swaying dagger-dance; slowly she drew the jade-hilted blade from its silver sheath, and then once more the pace quickened and she began to sway and leap with blazing eyes, pointing her dagger now here, now there, striking the air like a warrior surrounded by enemies.

Now the rhythm quickened to fever pace, faster and faster she whirled, closer and closer she came to the men as they sat as if under an enchantment, and then at last, with a sudden movement, she plunged her dagger into the heart of Hussein!

In horror at such a deed, Ali Baba and his son started up, but there she stood before them, panting and wiping the dripping blade of her dagger.

'Look!' said she, and shuddered as she fixed her eyes on the lifeless body. Then they saw that the long, venerable silver beard had slipped aside and revealed black, hoggish bristles and a cruel face that was by now only too well known to Ali Baba!

'The oil-merchant! The robber-captain!' he cried. Then he took Morgiana to his breast and, kissing her between the eyes, he exclaimed, 'Blessed child! Light of my eyes! Be my daughter in very truth! Marry this handsome son of mine!'

Now Morgiana had long secretly loved Ahmad, her master's son, and it seemed to Ahmad, now that he had seen Morgiana in her sudden blaze of beauty and courage, that no fate could be more fortunate than to marry such a wonderful girl.

And so, not long after, Ahmad and Morgiana were married, but not before Ali Baba had buried the robber-chief in the grave which hid the rest of his cruel band.

For a long time Morgiana, who had saved them and who was slow to forget the dangers that they had all survived, begged her young husband and Ali Baba not to visit the treasure-cave again. Ali Baba had told her that there had once been forty thieves and, not knowing that two had been beheaded by the captain's own hand, she begged them both to consider that there might very likely still be danger.

But time passed and, at last, Ali Baba and his son persuaded the prudent Morgiana to come with them to the cave. As they went, she saw for herself that the path had become quite overgrown, not only with grasses, but with woody shrubs, and that now, long creepers hung down in front of what had once been the split in the rock. Then even the careful Morgiana agreed that no one could have passed that way for a very long time and that Allah, in his mercy, had somehow ended their danger.

So now, once more, Ali Baba—this time with his son and Morgiana—stood before the rock. Once more he called out in a firm voice, *'Open Sesame!'*

And then, for the first time, the two young people went in and saw the vastness of the treasure which was to be their inheritance.

'Glory be to Allah who gives abundance beyond counting to the humble!' exclaimed Ali Baba once more, and once more he took only a few sacks of gold and precious stones.

And so they all lived for many years in peace and happiness, taking care not to excite the envy of the neighbours by too sudden prosperity, but, instead, earning blessings by their kindness to the poor and their hospitality to strangers.

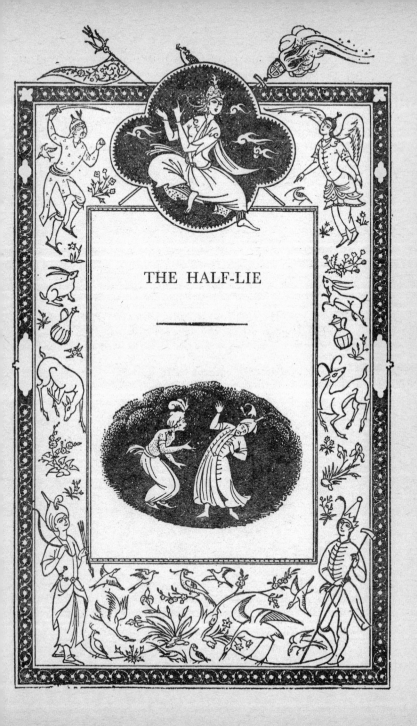

THE HALF-LIE

A merchant was one day walking through the market in Cairo when he saw a negro slave for sale.

'How much is this slave?' he asked.

'Only six hundred pieces of silver,' replied the slave dealer, 'for he has a single fault.'

'What's that?' said the merchant.

'Why,' said the slave dealer, 'he always tells one lie a year, and, if you buy him, you must put up with one lie each year.'

Now the merchant loved a bargain. 'Only one lie a year?' thought he. 'That isn't much! Most slaves tell many more. So do I, for that matter.' So he bought Kafur, as the slave was called, took him home and set him to work, and for some months all went well. Kafur was cheerful and obedient, and worked hard.

On New Year's Day the merchant and some of his friends rode out on their mules to a pretty flower garden a little way outside the city to celebrate. They took wine and fruit and sweet cakes with them, carpets to sit on, and musical instruments. Kafur went with them.

About midday the merchant said to Kafur, 'Mount my mule and ride home. Ask my wife for more pistachio nuts and bring them back as fast as you can.'

Kafur set off. But as he drew near the merchant's house he tore his clothes and began to howl out loud, 'Oh, my master,' he sobbed, 'oh, my poor master! What will become of us all now?'

Many people—old and young—heard and gathered round him, and they all went along with him to his master's house. When the merchant's wife heard Kafur's cries and howls, and saw the crowd of people, she ran to the door.

'O mistress!' screamed the slave, the tears running down his face. 'My poor master is dead! The old garden wall, in whose shade he was sitting with his friends, fell suddenly and killed them all!'

Then the merchant's wife wept too, and tore her clothes; and so did his daughters and all the women of the house, and all the women in the crowd ran in to comfort them. The merchant's wife ran through her home and, in sign of despair, she began breaking the windows and smashing the china—just to show how much she loved her husband, for that was how people often showed sorrow when the master of the house was dead.

'Come, Kafur, and help me mourn!' called out the merchant's wife, and between them they pulled down shelves, broke crockery, tore the rich hangings and smeared soot on the walls. Bang! went a blue and gold china coffee-pot upon the floor. Crash! and Kafur, with a sob, hurled his master's precious coffee cups

through the window. Smash! he threw a little ebony table inlaid with ivory after the coffee cups so that it broke in pieces in the courtyard, and all the while Kafur kept calling out, 'Oh, my poor master! my poor master!'

Kafur and the merchant's wife tore the gold embroidered cushions and ripped up the divans. Kafur, with a great tug, pulled down the high shelves which ran round the kitchen just under the roof, and clatter bang! all the green and blue china and silver and gold bowls on them fell to the floor and broke.

Kafur worked with a will, and ran all over the house, till soon the whole place looked like a ruin, with broken china, soot and torn stuff everywhere.

'Now,' said the merchant's wife, 'let us go and fetch my poor husband's body!' So she ran out of the house, with all the women and slaves following her, and as

they went through the streets more and more people began to join in, while one of the neighbours made the crowd still bigger by running to tell the Governor of the city, who immediately sent workmen to the garden with picks and baskets to dig out the bodies.

Kafur ran in front of them all, still howling and weeping and crying out, 'Oh my poor master, my poor master!' Soon he had outdistanced all the others, so that he got first to the garden, with the huge crowd some way behind. Then, though he still howled and wept, he began to cry out:

'Oh woe, woe! Oh my mistress! My mistress! Who will care for me now?'

Soon his master, who was sitting peacefully with his friends, heard him.

'What's this?' said the merchant, standing up and looking very pale. 'In Allah's name, what has happened?'

'Ah, Master,' said Kafur, 'when I reached your house I found that it had fallen down, and that everyone inside it had been killed.'

'My wife?' said the merchant.

'Dead,' cried Kafur.

'And the mule I loved to ride on?'

'Crushed, too,' cried Kafur.

'And my son and my daughters?'

'All dead,' cried Kafur. 'And the sheep and the geese and the hens too! Cats and dogs are eating them even now.'

Then the merchant beat his breast and tore his fine clothes. His friends, when they heard, wept too, and they all started off towards the city.

They had not gone far when, of course, they met the merchant's wife and family, the huge crowd of neighbours and the workmen who had been sent by the Governor.

'Oh, my love, are you safe?' cried the merchant's wife.

'Oh, my life, how is it with you?' cried the merchant.

'Why, we are all right,' said his wife. 'But Kafur came weeping and with his clothes torn and told us the wall of the garden had fallen upon you as you feasted!'

'No!' said the merchant; 'Kafur ran in here, weeping and crying, clothes torn and with dust on his head, and told us the house had fallen upon you and that you were all killed!'

Then they both turned on Kafur, who was still weeping and crying and beating his breast.

'How's this, you wretch?' said the merchant. 'You black ill-omened son of the Evil One! You won't get off lightly, I can tell you! Just wait till we get home, and then you'll have a beating you won't forget.'

'Oh no, master!' answered Kafur with a grin. 'That would not be fair! You bought me cheap because I had one fault, and you said you would put up with the consequences of my telling one lie a year. So far this has only been half a lie! Before the end of the year I'll tell the other half.'

The merchant was furious. But, all the same, all the bystanders agreed that it would not be fair for him to punish Kafur. But when he got home and found his house in such a state, and so much damage done, he remembered with horror that Kafur had talked about more lies before the year was out.

'Do you call all this only half a lie?'

'Yes, master!' said Kafur, grinning.

'Why, then, a whole lie of yours would wreck a city, or even two! You're not going to tell the other half here, I can tell you! I'd rather set you free! Be off out of my house at once!'

So Kafur became a free man, but he was a lazy fellow and knew no trade, and with no master to set him to work he lived as best he could as a beggar, and often went hungry.

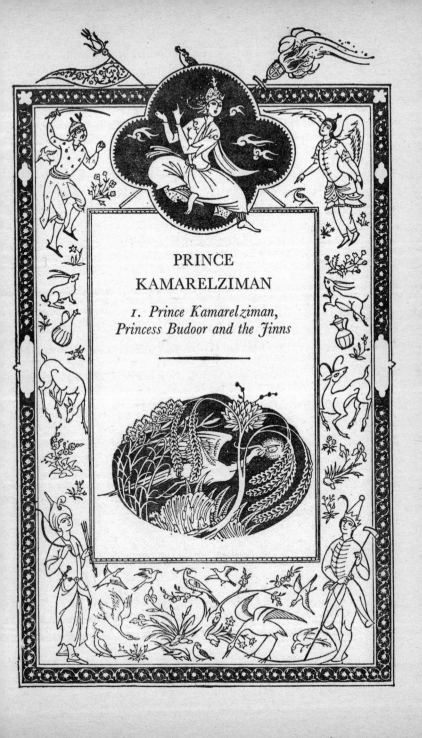

PRINCE
KAMARELZIMAN

*I. Prince Kamarelziman,
Princess Budoor and the Jinns*

There lived once long ago among the islands of Khalidan, not far from Persia, a Sultan who had one son.

He was old, and though his son Prince Kamarelziman was still little more than a boy, the Sultan, wishing the succession to the throne to be made sure, told the young Prince that it was time for him to take a wife.

To his surprise, the charming young Prince only hung his head and said:

'O my Father, do not order me to marry! It is true that I owe you obedience, but I have read so much of the wickedness of women that I cannot endure the idea. Women, as is well known, are the cause of all calamities and misfortunes!'

The Sultan was not pleased with this answer, but his Vizier advised that, as the Prince was so young, he should be given time.

After some months the Sultan called Kamarelziman again, and again he told him that it was time for him to marry.

'But I have read,' the young Prince pleaded, 'that women are so cunning that, though a man should build a thousand castles of iron and lead, all this will be of no use! With their fingers dyed with henna, and their hair arranged in plaits, with their painted eyelids and their false smiles, I am sure that they bring nothing but misfortune!'

Again the Vizier advised the angry Sultan to have patience.

'See, O mighty Sultan, how every day the young Prince grows more and more charming! Time, with the blessing of Allah, will also make him grow more obedient and sensible.'

The third time, instead of speaking privately as before, the Sultan called Kamarelziman before the throne and spoke in front of all the Emirs and grave counsellors and impetuous warriors.

'Before this great assembly,' said the Sultan, 'I command you to do your duty and to marry a daughter of some neighbouring King, so that the royal line shall not die out! Otherwise the succession to my throne will not be safe and peaceful!'

But the young Prince only looked wildly about him and, flushing hotly, in the foolishness of his youth exclaimed before them all:

'O my Father, your words are foolish and I will not obey you! I have already declared this! No! I will not marry even if you make me drink the cup of perdition!'

At that the Sultan was very angry, for he felt that his son had not only defied him in front of all the grave counsellors, mighty lords and impetuous soldiers, but had spoken most rudely. So he shouted out loudly in his wrath:

'Do not dare to answer me with such insolence, O disobedient son! Hitherto you have never known punishment nor anger! Now learn what it is to disobey a Sultan and a Father!' With that the guards were ordered to seize Kamarelziman and lock him into a dark room without windows at the top of a high tower of the royal castle. The Sultan ordered them to give him only a couch, a coverlet, a lantern and a pillow, and to post a guard at the door.

'How wretched am I,' thought the young Prince when the door had been shut upon him. 'A curse on marriage and girls and deceitful women! It is because of women that I have brought shame upon myself.'

So there he sat alone all day, repenting of having spoken so rudely. He tried to pass the long day in reciting chapters of the Koran aloud—the chapter

68

called 'The Cow', and another called 'The Compassionate'.

At last, when night came, some food was brought him and, having eaten, but still with a heavy heart, the young Prince fell asleep.

Now this castle tower was very old and had not been used for many years and in its foundations was a well that had been dug in the time of the ancient Romans. It chanced that, in this well, lived a Jinneeyeh—a female Jinnee—named Meymooneh, who was a great one of her tribe, for she was no less than the daughter of one of the Kings of the Jinns. She had heard the recitation of the Koran and now, in the night, when all was quiet, she came up from her well and was surprised to see light in the room at the top of the tower.

She found that the door of the old deserted room was shut and that a guard slept on the threshold. Naturally such things as guards and shut doors meant nothing to

Meymooneh and, entering the room, she saw a charming young man asleep on a couch.

She took up the lantern to see him better and was amazed at his beauty. She saw that his clothes and the covers on his bed were of silk, and felt that it must have been his voice that had recited the Koran so melodiously.

'By Allah!' said she to herself (for she was one of the Believing Jinns). 'This is the most beautiful young man that I have ever seen! His voice was as charming as his looks! How could his family have left him deserted in this lonely place? I am sure that there is not his like in the world!'

She bent down and heard that Kamarelziman was muttering in his sleep, 'Do not force me to marry, O my Father! Do not punish me!'

'So he will not marry! Alas that womankind should be deprived of him!' said the Jinneeyeh to herself, and she stood with her great wings folded, gazing at him. At last, setting down the lantern, after giving him a farewell kiss between the eyes, she flew through the roof of the tower. Spreading her great wings and rising high into the air, she soon heard near her the beating of other wings and, flying near, saw that this other pair belonged to a certain less powerful Jinn.

'Hurt me not, mighty Princess!' called he, seeing her poised above him like an eagle about to strike. 'It is only Dahnesh!'

Hearing him speak so respectfully, she flew lower.

'Where do you come from, Dahnesh?' she called.

'I come, O powerful Lady, from the islands that border China,' he answered.

'What did you see there?'

'The exquisite Budoor, daughter of the King of the Seven Palaces. Alas, her Father is offended with her and has imprisoned her. Yet Allah never created a human being so beautiful!'

'A fig for your princess, O stupid Dahnesh!' she called back. 'Come down here! I will show you a young man much better than she can be. It is he, not she, who is the most beautiful of all human beings.'

With that both Jinns came flying down and entered the tower. There they stood, one on each side of Kamarelziman's bed.

'See now!' said Meymooneh. 'His eyelashes are like silk!'

'Her eyelashes are like the wings of moths!' answered Dahnesh.

'His hair is as dark as the wing of a raven and his forehead as white as a pearl.'

71

'Budoor's hair is as black as clouds at midnight and her forehead is like the moon!'

'His lips are like coral.'

'Hers are like rubies.'

'His wrists are as delicate as lily stems and as strong as whipcord.'

'Budoor's little feet are so small that it is a wonder! Yet she walks more gracefully on them than a fawn.'

And so they went on.

'She must have a most disagreeable disposition,' said the Jinneeyeh at last, 'or her father would certainly not have shut her up, as you say.'

'That is only because she refuses to marry, O powerful Lady! She has no liking for men, but says that they are the cause of all the evil in the world, and so her father declares that she is mad. I go every night to gaze upon her while she sleeps!'

'If she is asleep now, you had better fetch her here immediately!' said the Jinneeyeh. 'We will put them side by side on this very couch and compare them. Then you will soon see that I am right.'

At that Dahnesh spread his wings and flew away, and was soon back carrying the sleeping princess and, when the two Jinns had laid them side by side, they saw that they were both exquisitely lovely and so much alike that it seemed impossible to decide which was the more elegant and charming! So still one Jinn praised Kamarelziman and the other praised Budoor. Though Dahnesh hated to give in, he was secretly afraid of Meymooneh, so he said:

'Let us, O Lady, call up Kashkash, the oldest of all Jinns, to decide.'

So Meymooneh stamped her foot, and at once Kashkash, oldest of all Jinns, appeared. Meymooneh and Dahnesh were comely and their wings were like those

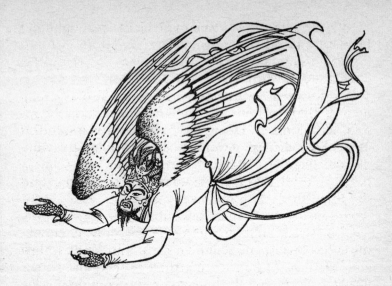

of rare birds, but Kashkash was hideous with age. He had seven horns on his head, slit eyes, and a skin like a crocodile's.

'Judge, O Kashkash!' said Meymooneh. 'Look carefully at these two young sleepers and say which of them is the most beautiful!'

For a long time Kashkash looked out of his slit eyes and declared solemnly that this prince and princess were equal in beauty and together were the wonder of the world.

'But you are here to decide, O Kashkash,' objected Meymooneh, frowning.

'Then wake them in turn, powerful Lady!' he answered. 'We shall see then which will behave the most discreetly and lovingly.'

Knowing that Budoor hated men and Kamarelziman hated women, neither of the two Jinns much liked this suggestion. However, there was no help, for they had agreed to abide by Kashkash's judgment.

73

So (the other two making themselves invisible) Dahnesh at once transformed himself into a flea and bit Prince Kamarelziman in a soft place on his neck, so that he woke with a cry.

What was the Prince's surprise to find that, though he was still in prison, a lovely girl was sleeping by his side. Rising on his elbow, he gazed at her and all his ideas of the vileness of women began to fly away and to dissolve like black clouds before the sun, and soon he began to think that this girl was surely the most exquisite thing that Allah had ever made.

'Speak to me, O most beautiful!' said he. But, say what he would, implore her as he might, he could not rouse her from her enchanted sleep and he was filled with despair. At last, fearing that, in the morning, he would believe that all this had only been a dream, he decided that he would try to find something that would prove that it had been real.

Catching sight of a curious ring on one of her fingers, he took it off and slipped it on to his own. No sooner had he done this than Meymooneh touched him with one of her wings and the young Prince fell at once into an enchanted sleep.

Now it was Budoor's turn. Dahnesh, still in the likeness of a flea, bit her as hard as he was able. When she opened her eyes and sat up, she saw to her astonishment that she was in a strange place and that a young man was sleeping by her side. But, though at first she felt frightened, as the young man neither spoke nor stirred, she soon plucked up courage and began to look closely at him.

Now this charming Princess had always lived secluded in one of her father's seven palaces and, except her father and an older foster-brother of hers, she had never seen a man close to. But now, there beside her,

74

lay the most elegant of young princes fast asleep. Long she looked and, as she looked, she began to doubt if men could really be as strange and odious as she had always declared that they were. This was not a long-bearded tyrant, but someone who seemed as young and innocent as herself. Soon she had fallen deep in love with him.

'O beloved of my heart!' she said softly. 'Wake from your sleep! O jewel among Princes, let me hear your voice.'

But, of course, all her coaxing was no use, for the Jinns had cast him into an enchanted sleep. At last Budoor decided, just as Kamarelziman had done, that (in case later on she should believe that this had all been a dream) she would take something from him that would be a proof that it had been real, so, in her turn, she took a ring from his finger and put it on her own. As she did so, what was her amazement to notice that, on his other hand, was her own ring! But Dahnesh did not give her another instant in which to think what this might mean, but immediately put her to sleep again.

By now the night was almost gone, so Kashkash declared that there was no longer time to make a judgment on such a difficult case!

'These young creatures have now, it is clear, given up their foolish ideas, and each has been equally loving to the other. I will myself carry the Princess back,' went on the old Jinn, 'for no harm must come to these two beautiful works of Allah. And do you two,' added he to Meymooneh and Dahnesh, 'cease to quarrel and wrangle! One of them is a boy and there-fore preferred by you, O powerful Lady! One is a girl and therefore preferred by Dahnesh! Allah made each lovely, but which of us can compare male and female? They are made for one another.'

2. Kamarelziman, Budoor and the Search

Now whether it was because they had other business high in the air, or because, in his wisdom, Allah forbade them to meddle any further in such affairs, or because they were neither of them pleased with the judgment given by old Kashkash, what is certain is that neither Jinn nor Jinneeyeh came any more either to the Prince or the Princess.

So now, therefore, since the Princess had been carried back to her home on the islands that border China, the distance which separated the lovers was so great that neither could get any news of the other.

In his castle the Sultan of Khalidan soon felt more worried than ever about his son because, though, indeed, Kamarelziman was perfectly willing to marry, he now declared that he would only marry the exquisite girl who had slept by his side on the night of his imprisonment.

'But it was a dream, my son!' the Sultan would assure him. 'The guard at your door heard and saw nothing! There is no window, so there can have been no beautiful girl!'

At that Prince Kamarelziman would only shake his head and point to the strange ring which was still on his finger. Soon he began to refuse food and to waste away because no one could find his beloved.

As for Princess Budoor, when she began to tell her father that she had changed her mind about the evil nature of men and was quite willing to marry, but then when she refused one King's son after another, he felt surer than ever that his unfortunate daughter was mad! Indeed, to prevent the fury of her suitors whom he had to refuse, he made a public proclamation that she was mad and therefore could marry no one. And so things might have gone on—the Prince growing more and more love-sick, and the Princess—far away —shut up for mad by her father.

Fortunately, however, the Princess's older foster-brother was very fond of her. Coming back from a journey, he heard the King's proclamation which said that the Princess Budoor was mad and, not believing it, he hurried to the palace and soon persuaded their old nurse to smuggle him in disguise into the women's apartments.

'Oh my sister!' he said, horrified and throwing off his disguise. 'It grieves my heart to see you chained as if you were a madwoman!'

'It is not madness, dear brother,' said she, 'unless it is madness to love the most beautiful young prince in the world!' So, then and there, she told him the whole story, described the room in which she had found herself, told him that, for a moment, she had seen her own ring on the young prince's finger, and then showed him the ring she had taken and that it bore the writing of a distant land. 'Since then my heart has been breaking for the sight of this Prince!' added she sadly.

'I agree with you that this was not a dream!' said her foster-brother, examining the ring. 'And I am also sure there is no other cure for you, dear sister, than for you to be reunited to your young prince. Do not despair! I was about to set out on my travels again, and now I shall do so immediately and inquire in every city for this princely young man.'

True to his word, he set out and, for a month, he journeyed, but could hear no word or clue that might lead him to a country whose inhabitants wrote such characters as those on the ring, or whose garments, or the furnishing of whose rooms, were such as Budoor had described.

At last, in a distant city, he heard that, among the islands of Khalidan, lived a Sultan whose only son was dying for the love of an unknown lady and that a ring was the only token he had of her.

Setting sail, he had almost reached the shores of Khalidan when a terrible wind began to blow. This wind, and the great waves that it soon roused, carried away his sail, and finally broke the ship's mast, whose fall swamped the ship.

Now it so happened that the Sultan had taken his almost dying son to a certain palace close to the seashore in the hope that the cool air might make him better. Looking out of the palace window, one of the attendants saw the shipwreck and then a man struggling in the water, and begged leave of the Sultan, who sat by his son's bedside, to go down and help this poor stranger to the shore.

It was by this means that, when he had recovered a little and the Sultan sending for him, Budoor's foster-brother found himself face to face with a beautiful young man who seemed indeed to be a young prince and who, pale and wan, lay upon a couch on a terrace above the sea. Now it happened that the hand of the sick young man lay upon the embroidered coverlet of the couch and on one of the fingers was a curious ring that Budoor's foster-brother thought he recognized.

However, he was too prudent to show his surprise, for by the side of the bed sat the old Sultan, who looked sternly at him.

'Who are you, stranger?' asked the old Sultan. 'And what is your profession? And why do you come un-invited to our palace?'

Bowing low, the foster-brother answered that he was a poet, but had also, in his travels, learned some skill in curing those who were sick.

'Allow me, oh mighty Sultan,' added he, 'to while

away the time by reciting a few verses, for, as is said, the words of poets are sometimes the healers of souls.'

Now the Sultan was tired of all the doctors and magicians who kept coming to the palace without number, for none had been able to do anything for his son. However, he thought that a poem could do no harm.

'Speak then!' said the Sultan.

The foster-brother began to consider. He thought that perhaps, through a poem, he might give a riddling message which would only be understood if this was indeed the young Prince who was loved by Budoor, so he began:

> 'Alas for the Prince who is wounded by love,
> His wound is one hard to heal.
> Of her eyes the arrows pierced as deep
> As those shot from a bow of steel.
> But the bow of steel in sleep
> Wounded her who now mourns like a dove
> Who knows no more of her love
> Than the circle of a ring
> Till the circle of love be done
> And he and she find healing
> In giving kisses and sealing
> A faith that can make them one.'

Neither the Sultan nor those who stood by could make anything of these odd verses, but they all noticed that a new light seemed to have come into the eyes of the young Prince, who, almost too weak to speak, made a sign to the Sultan that the stranger should be allowed to come nearer. Unfortunately the Sultan, though he was overjoyed to see that his son seemed to have enjoyed the verses, remained sitting with them, and so for a long time neither the Prince nor Budoor's foster-brother thought it prudent to speak of what was in their hearts. All the Prince could do was to keep playing with the Princess' ring in such a way that the stranger could get a good look at it. But now the Prince spoke for the first time for many days and asked for a little food, saying that he would eat with this excellent poet.

Still the Sultan stayed, glad to see that his son had at last eaten a little rice and fish.

At last Kamarelziman pretended that he wanted to sleep, but asked that the strange poet might remain beside him so that, if he awoke, he might be able to soothe him to sleep again with more verses. So at last the Sultan left them and, the attendants taking up the couch, the Prince and the stranger retired to Kamarelziman's room.

As soon as they were alone, Kamarelziman sat up and, with his eyes shining, asked the meaning of the riddling verses about 'rings' and 'sleep' and 'love'. As he heard the story, the Prince felt more and more sure that his own mysterious lady really must be this exquisite Budoor, daughter of The King of the Seven Palaces and foster-sister of the man before him. What excited him most was to learn that all that he himself had suffered from love had also been felt by the lovely girl. Kamarelziman's terrible weakness gradually began to leave him and he rose from his bed and began to pace about the room.

'There is no longer any doubt in my mind,' said the stranger when Kamarelziman had described his own ring, 'that you, O Prince, are my foster-sister's lost love and that Budoor is your lady!'

So then they began to discuss what was to be done, for Kamarelziman felt sure that the Sultan, his father, would be most unwilling to allow his only son to go on a long and dangerous journey. They decided that in the morning the Prince was still to seem to be weak and weary, but to seem to recover gradually but only to feel better when the stranger was near, and that they should both pretend that this was not only in consequence of the reciting of poems, but also of spells or herbs.

So, after a few days of this, and when the Prince had let it seem that he was almost strong again, he asked leave of the Sultan to go hunting in the desert and to take the stranger with him.

'Go then,' answered the Sultan, 'but stay away no more than one night, for I shall miss you sorely and also I cannot believe that you are more than partly recovered.'

Under pretence of needing much food and water and a tent, they loaded a camel with necessities for a long journey, and the two of them mounted the best horses in the Sultan's stable. Unfortunately the Sultan ordered six of his mounted guards to go with them.

However, during the hunt, they made pretence of chasing a particular gazelle and managed, taking the baggage-camel, to get away from the guards. Then, as soon as they were out of sight, they abandoned the hunt and made off as quickly as they could in the direction of the kingdom of The King of the Seven Palaces.

Long did they travel, over both land and sea, and many times, when some new city came in sight, did

Kamarelziman ask, 'Is it this?' But each time Budoor's foster-brother would shake his head. At last there came a time when he answered:

'It lies before us, O Prince!'

Now, as her foster-brother already knew, Princess Budoor was kept shut away in the women's part of the palace, and to these apartments her father would certainly not have admitted any young man who seemed in the least like a suitor.

They had spoken often of this difficulty as they travelled and decided that the only way in which the young Prince could hope to see Budoor was to disguise himself as a doctor, but that it would be best first to smuggle in a letter which would prepare Budoor. The letter would explain that, though the doctor was not a doctor, yet this was not some new trick planned by the King her father to coax her into marriage.

So now, in the city, they lodged in the Khan or rest-house of the merchants, and there Prince Kamarelziman wrote his letter.

'This letter,' he began, 'is from the tormented heart of the distracted, the distressed, the passionate, the perplexed Kamarelziman, son of the Sultan of Khalidan, who has not ceased to be the captive and slave of the incomparable Princess Budoor. I send you, lovely lady, your ring which has been my only consolation since I took it in exchange when we were together. O lady more lovely than the dawn, send me back mine in token of your kindness!'

This letter, some elegant and loving verses, and the ring, they managed to get smuggled into the women's apartments in which Budoor sat chained and, as they had planned, the letter reached her just in time for her to have read it at the moment when the pretended doctor had been allowed to stand outside her room. No sooner had she seen that it was indeed her own ring and finished reading the letter than, with a mighty effort, she broke the silver chains that bound her, pushed aside the curtain and, holding out his ring, stood before the dazzled Kamarelziman in all her radiant joy.

The happiness of the lovers can be imagined, and indeed they were so joyful that they almost forgot that they still had The King of the Seven Palaces to reckon with. Fortunately Budoor's foster-brother had remembered this and had been busy telling the King about his journey, and had taken care to say how splendid was the Court of the Sultan of Khalidan, and about how a certain young prince, of incomparable beauty, was the heir to the kingdom.

So, when the Prince and Princess prostrated themselves before the King, and when he had heard the whole story, he forgave them for Kamarelziman's deception in getting to see Budoor by pretending to be a doctor. The marriage was celebrated immediately and, for a whole month, there was nothing but feasting and rejoicing in The Kingdom of the Seven Palaces.

What befell after that happy time shall be told in the Story of Kamarelziman, Budoor and the Ebony Islands.

3. Kamarelziman, Budoor and the Ebony Islands

Now the Sultan of Khalidan had loved his only son, and the Prince had, as yet, found no means of letting him know of his happiness and good fortune, and so it happened that, after a while, Kamarelziman began to be troubled every night with dreams in which it seemed to him that he saw the unhappiness of his father and indeed that the whole kingdom of Khalidan was plunged in mourning.

Budoor, noticing his trouble, asked him the cause of it and, when she heard it, they agreed that she should go to her father, the King, and ask leave for Kamarelziman to go and pay the old Sultan a visit. The King was not very willing, but at last he consented. What was far harder was to get him to let Budoor go, too. But she pleaded with him so prettily, and declared so sadly that, if they were once again separated, she would probably die, that, at last, he gave in.

So the Prince and Princess set out on the long journey. The King provided them with a train of camels, mules and horses loaded with tents and all they would need, with a splendid mule-litter for the Princess in which she could lie shaded by curtains if she felt tired, and, of course, with splendid presents for the Sultan of Khalidan.

For a whole month they travelled, through deserts and across mountains, camping each night.

One evening, their tents were pitched in a pleasant meadow, and here, since they had spent many days and nights in desert places, they were glad to rest under the shade of cool trees and with the sound of water and of the song of birds in their ears. There was grass for the animals and wood to cook their evening meal, and Kamarelziman and Budoor were weary after a whole month of journeying.

In the morning, very early, before anyone else in the camp was astir, Prince Kamarelziman woke, but the Princess and all the attendants still slept. Standing by the Princess as she lay, Kamarelziman noticed that, near her hand, tied into the band of the muslin

85

trousers that she wore, was a red jewel that he had not noticed before. He did not doubt that this must be some talisman or lucky stone that she valued. There seemed to be writing on the jewel, but it was rather dark in the tent, so, curious to see if he could read the inscription, he took it outside to look at it more closely. No sooner had he come out of the tent than a large bird swooped down and snatched the jewel out of his hand.

Feeling sure that the stone must be precious to his dear Budoor, Kamarelziman was after the bird in a moment, for it had not flown right away, but had alighted again on the ground. The bird did not take wing but only fluttered and hopped, fluttered and hopped, in front of him, so that Kamarelziman felt sure that he would soon be able to catch it. But now, the faster he ran, the faster went the bird. Up hill and down dale went the thievish bird with the Prince after it, till at last, just as the sun was setting, the wretched thief suddenly flew up to the top of a high tree far out of reach. Looking round him, Kamarelziman remembered with horror that he had left the camp without a

word to anyone and had spent the whole day chasing the bird. Now he saw that, worse still, he was now completely lost and had no idea in which direction he must go to find Budoor again. It was now too dark to see to walk at all or to see what had become of the bird, so, hungry, thirsty, and bitterly repenting his foolish conduct, poor Kamarelziman lay down under the tree.

Meantime, of course, Budoor had long been awake and was not only surprised but very much grieved and alarmed at finding her husband gone. She wondered what she should do. It seemed to her that she was indeed in great danger.

'If I go and tell the guards that the Prince has gone, they might easily decide to take all our treasure and even carry me off to sell as a slave.'

Now she remembered that they still had the curtained litter with them in which, if the Princess was weary, she could rest and be carried by the mules in a kind of curtained bed. So now she told one of her slave girls that, during the next part of the journey, she herself would ride and that the girl could take her place

in the curtained litter. That done, she put on some of Kamarelziman's clothes and, as men often do in the desert to keep the dust out of their mouths and nostrils,  she wound a second scarf round one of his turbans in such a way that it hid part of her face. Then, imitating Kamarelziman's way of speaking, she told the attendants and guards that they had decided to stay one more day in that pleasant place in order to rest the animals. What she hoped was, of course, that, if they did not move off at once the Prince would find them more easily. All that day and the next night she waited. But at last, with a heavy heart, she disguised herself again, called out the guards and muleteers and, as Kamarelziman had done on other days, gave her orders as to how the loads were to be distributed. She was an excellent rider and she had disguised her voice so that, as they rode slowly on their way, no one suspected that this was not the real Kamarelziman and that the lady in the curtained litter was not Budoor. It can be imagined that they now travelled slowly and that, in case he should somehow come up with them, Budoor was careful to leave word in every village through which they went and with every horseman they chanced to meet that it was the caravan of the Prince Kamarelziman and the Princess Budoor that had passed that way. But in truth poor Budoor knew not whether it would be best to go forward or back, so that her heart was heavy.

At last they came in sight of the sea and of a great city. This was the capital of the Islands of Ebony, which lay on a tongue of the mainland. She knew that

88

this city was on the way to Khalidan and, because of that, she decided to make a stay there if she could, so, not far from the city, she ordered their camp to be pitched. This would, she thought, be a place in which Prince Kamarelziman would be likely to enquire for her.

Now the King of that country was a courteous old man and, when he saw their encampment, he sent a messenger to invite the young Prince, who seemed to be the leader, to come to his palace. Princess Budoor, still in her man's dress and still giving herself out to be Prince Kamarelziman, came, and was graciously received. Indeed her reception was altogether too gracious. In fact, it was not long before the old King, taking a sudden fancy to this charming young man, invited her to marry his daughter and to become King in his stead!

What was Budoor to do? She was afraid that if she confessed that she had deceived him, the old King of the Ebony Isles might well feel foolish, and that, if he felt foolish, he would very likely also feel angry and then, if she tried to get back to her camp and then push on towards Khalidan, he might possibly send an army after them and kill them all.

It seemed to her that the least dangerous plan might be to pretend to agree and then, when they were alone together throw herself on the mercy of this daughter of his, a girl whom she had never seen.

'If she will so much as consent to hear my story, surely any girl might pity me?'

But, as can be guessed, it was with a heavy heart that poor Budoor attended the wedding rejoicings and took her seat on the throne of the Ebony Isles.

At last, as soon as she was alone with Amina en Nufoos—for that was the name of the King's daughter —Budoor, to the girl's amazement, threw herself at her feet, weeping and begging her help! Amina could not imagine what help was needed by this charming young man, and her wonder increased as Budoor told her the story.

'O my sister,' ended Budoor, 'turn the eye of mercy and kindness on me! In the name of Allah I beg you to keep my secret!'

Upon that Amina put her arms round Budoor and comforted her, and so, alone together, they passed the time in kindness as if they had indeed been sisters.

And now every day Budoor sat upon the throne and did justice and levied or remitted taxes and settled the affairs of the army and the merchants. But of all those who lived in that whole city only Princess Amina knew Budoor's secret, and with her alone Budoor could rest from her long pretence.

Now, as has been said, both Kamarelziman and Budoor, though they had lost each other, still both knew one thing. This was that this kingdom of the Ebony Isles was on the way to Khalidan. So the lost Kamarelziman was trying to find his way there, just as the forsaken Budoor had planned to wait there, for that seemed to each the best hope.

It happened that, as he travelled, Kamarelziman came to a certain city of the Magians—the Fire and Sun worshippers—which was ruled by a violent King who hated True Believers. Indeed, if it had not been for a good old man who was a gardener, and who lived just outside the place, it might have gone hard with Kamarelziman, for he was a pious young man and every day he repeated the morning, noon-day and evening prayers that are pleasing to Allah, and so he would soon, without thinking, have revealed his faith. Indeed the old gardener, who was himself a secret Moslem, recognized him at once as a True Believer.

'Why do you come to this dangerous city, O my son?' asked the old gardener as soon as he had Kamarelziman hidden safe in his house. Then, little by little, Kamarelziman told his story and how now the only hope he had of finding his lost Princess was to get to the Ebony Islands.

'We have all heard of the Ebony Isles,' said the gardener. 'But alas, there is only one ship in every year that trades there, and that ship has just sailed. So you must now wait for many months. Allah will grant you patience, my son!'

Now Kamarelziman was a prince who had had power over treasures and slaves, so that his first thought was to get a special ship for himself. Then he remembered that he was now poor, in fact utterly without money, and, very humbly, the Prince begged the old man to let him work for him in the garden just for food and shelter till the ship sailed. To this the good old gardener agreed with pleasure, for it was long since he had had one of his own faith to talk to.

And so the Prince stayed in the garden, working with hoe and basket, or opening or shutting off the rills that watered the fruit trees. He helped with all the old

man's concerns, cultivating the ground and gathering the crops whether of melons or of other fruits. But, though this garden was a pleasant place, his heart was heavy with sorrow at this long separation from his beloved Budoor.

One morning, when the old gardener was away selling the produce in the market, Kamarelziman, looking up, saw three strange birds who were fighting. They soared high into the air and he saw that two were attacking the third bird, and that presently, still on the wing, they killed it, ripping up its body. As the dead bird fell to the ground Kamarelziman saw something that shone, lying among the scattered feathers and the sprinkled blood. Going up to see what it was, he found to his astonishment that it was none other than the jewel that had been the cause of his absence from the camp and of the separation from Budoor. He recognized it at once and his heart was lightened.

'This is surely a good omen!' said he to himself. 'This is a sign that the time of our misfortune is drawing to an end.'

And so, indeed, it proved, for, no sooner had he begun his work again, loosening the ground round the roots of a tree which bore the long, sweet, black pods of the locust-bean, than he noticed that the blow of his hoe gave out an unusual hollow sound. Surprised at this, he scratched away the earth, found under it a trap-door and under that a treasure of gold stored in ancient leather jars. No sooner had he put back the trap-door and earth than he heard the old gardener's returning footsteps.

'Good news, my son!' called out the old man in a joyful tone. 'There is a ship now in the harbour which will sail in three days to the Islands of Ebony.'

Kamarelziman, delighted, embraced the old gardener and kissed his hand, and said that he also had good news, and told him how he had found a great treasure. The old gardener marvelled, for he, and his father before him, had cultivated that garden for eighty years and had found nothing.

'The treasure is yours, my son!' said he.

Nothing that Kamarelziman could say could persuade the kind old man to take more than a few of the gold pieces.

So, at last, Kamarelziman set sail with his treasure, having first, on the advice of the old gardener, hidden the gold by putting at the top of each jar a layer of fine ripe olives. Then, after a prosperous journey, they reached the chief city of the Ebony Isles where Budoor reigned as King.

Now it was Budoor's custom to question all the merchants whose ships put into the port, for she hoped in this way to get news of Kamarelziman. So, as usual, the master of the ship was brought before the throne.

'What merchandize have you on your ship?' asked she.

'I have spices, O mighty King, and sweet gums for incense, and medicinal herbs, aloe wood, and costly stuffs and tamarinds, and there is a merchant with me who has jars of splendid olives such as grow only in the country of the Fire Worshippers.'

Budoor decided to buy the olives and asked to which of the merchants in the ship they belonged. Kamarelziman himself was brought before the throne. She recognized him at once, but, as she sat in her dress as a King and high on a throne, he did not know her. Naturally Budoor longed for her beloved, but she said to herself that, in all this time, perhaps Kamarelziman's heart might have changed towards her. Besides, she knew she must be prudent, for she herself had deceived the old King of the Ebony Islands. If she acted hastily, she feared for the safety not only of herself and for Kamarelziman, but also for the kind Princess Amina. She owed her life to Amina, for she alone knew her secret and, for all these months, she had kept it well. Indeed, this Princess had now become dearer to Budoor than a sister.

So Budoor merely bargained for the olives, bought them, and gave out that she had taken a fancy to this charming and accomplished young merchant. Soon she began to show him every sort of honour, introducing him to the old King and keeping him constantly at her side.

All this greatly surprised Kamarelziman, who could not imagine why this young King should almost overwhelm him with kindness. At last he said to Budoor:

'O mighty King! You have bestowed on me favours innumerable, yet I have one favour left to ask you.'

'What is it?' asked the pretended king.

'Take back, noble young King, all that you have given me and let me go to my own country!'

'Foolish and ungrateful young man!' cried she, in pretended anger. 'Why do you want to rush headlong into all the dangers of travel, when, at my court, you have all that your heart could desire?'

'Alas!' cried he. 'My heart desires only one thing! Though you are like a Sun of goodness to me, my heart cannot know peace, for I have lost my only real treasure, my lovely and dear Princess Budoor. There is nothing in the world that can bring me pleasure or happiness except to find her again. It is for this reason only that I beg you to allow me to return to my own country, for it was to that place that we journeyed when I lost her and it may be that she is there.'

At that Budoor rejoiced greatly, for now at last she was sure that his heart was as true as her own. So, taking him by the hand, she led him to an apartment where they could be alone, and then all that day and the night that followed were not enough for their joy and for telling the history of what had happened to each of them. He told of the good old gardener and Budoor praised the kindness of Princess Amina, her pretended wife.

At last the time came when the whole tale must also be told to the old King, so Budoor, dressed once more as a Princess, and with Kamarelziman at her side, told it all. The old King was amazed, and as for Budoor her joy was only diminished when she told him that she supposed that now she would have to part with her dear loyal friend, Princess Amina.

'Need that be?' said the old Sultan at last. 'Does not the prophet allow four wives to the Faithful? Why, therefore, cannot this Prince have two?'

At this Budoor's heart was lightened and delight filled her, and, Kamarelziman and Princess Amina consenting gladly, the thing was done.

And this is the end of this strange tale.

The wisdom of Allah had now, as has been seen, decreed that Kamarelziman, the young Prince who had refused to marry because he said that all women were evil, should gladly marry two wives, who loved both him and each other, tenderly, and who had both performed good and eminent deeds, while Budoor, the young Princess, who had said that all men were evil, had for long not only loved a young man better than her life, but had herself taken the part of a man and a king. Kashkash, the old Jinnee, had indeed declared truly when he said that men and women are made for one another.

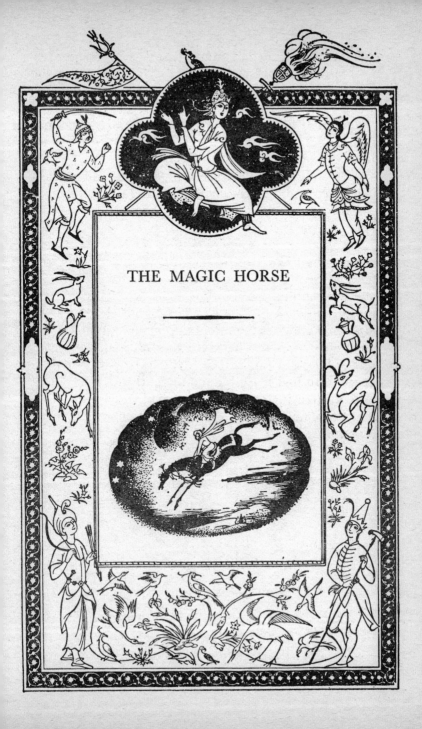

THE MAGIC HORSE

There was once, long ago, a King in Persia who loved philosophy and geometry, but even more, this King loved to be astonished. Anyone who brought to his court some new magical invention was sure to get a splendid reward, so that all sorts of magicians and inventors brought him their marvels, and soon his treasure-house was full of such things as trumpets that blew themselves, mechanical peacocks that spread their tails every hour to tell the time, and many other curiosities.

Such things were always brought to the King on the first day of a certain great feast that the Persians held every year, and all the people came out on holiday to see. It was always a fine sight, for the King would be out in the main square seated on his throne, he would be dressed in magnificent robes embroidered with many colours and he would wear on his head the glittering royal diadem, crowned with a shining image of the sun.

On one day, as the King sat on this gorgeous throne with his courtiers round him, he saw the crowd part and that a strange, ugly-looking old man was coming towards him.

The old man (who was a magician) was leading the figure of a great black horse, as large as a real horse, and as they came nearer the King saw that the horse was made of ebony and splendidly caparisoned. When he had kissed the ground before the King, the old magician spoke, telling him that this horse was able to fly with its rider through the air.

Now it was the King's custom never to accept any invention or to give any reward till he had seen with his own eyes that the invention would really work.

'Mount your horse then, O sage,' said the King,

'and bring me a leaf from one of the palm trees that grow at the foot of yonder mountain.'

The old magician bowed, mounted the horse, the horse flew into the air and, in a few moments they were back again and the strange-looking old man had laid the palm-leaf at the King's feet.

'What reward will you take for this marvel?' asked the delighted and astonished King.

'I must have two rewards, O most magnificent King,' answered the wizened old magician.

'Name them!' answered the King, looking at the magic horse with longing.

What was the horror of all who stood by, and especially of the young princes and princesses, when the hideous old magician said that he must not only have a great sum in gold, but also the hand of the King's youngest daughter in marriage!

'The first demand is easy,' answered the King, frowning. 'You shall have twice as much gold as you have asked for! Do not ask for the second!'

So they began to bargain, but all could soon tell that the King so much wanted the horse that he might perhaps be persuaded. However much the King's unfortunate young daughter wept, the old magician was not going to part with his horse unless he got her as well as the gold.

Now the King's son, Yusuf, the young Prince of Persia, who stood near his weeping sister, had been watching carefully and had seen that, when the magician had mounted the horse, he had put his hand to a sort of wooden peg, a turning-pin, on its neck. So, thinking that, if his precious horse was up in the sky, the horrible old man would be more likely to listen to reason, Prince Yusuf ran out from among the courtiers and guards, vaulted on to the horse and immediately

turned the pin. Whereupon the horse soared into the air as before, so that Prince and horse were soon out of sight.

Then a dreadful thought occurred to this bold young man. True, he had seen what the magician did to start the horse and to make it fly, but he had not been able to see what he did either to turn it or to make it come down again. Prince Yusuf pulled first one rein and then the other, trying to turn the horse's head. But still it flew straight on, mounting higher and higher, so that the air grew cold and soon the Prince could no longer so much as see the ground below him. How heartily he wished that he had not been so hasty! However, luckily, though he was certainly rash, he was also a sensible young man and, as well as he could— though they were still rushing through the air at a great speed—he began to feel about on the horse's neck and shoulders, supposing that whatever it was that turned the horse or made it come down, must be somewhere in reach of its rider. Presently he thought he felt a sort of knob on the horse's right shoulder and, putting his hand also on its left shoulder, felt that there was also another knob on that side.

So great was the speed with which the horse flew that he could hardly see out of his eyes. However, he bent down and at last saw that these knobs were neatly made in the shape of a cock's head. He thought he would try if they would turn, like the pin that made the horse fly. Turning the cock's head on the right shoulder, he found that the horse not only turned to the right but began to come down, while the same thing happened with the knob on the left.

Prince Yusuf's heart was filled with joy, for now that he had control of the flight, he was able to enjoy the wonderful sensation. He came lower now to admire the country over which they were passing. All was strange, and he saw rivers, mountains and cities that he had never seen before. About sunset he began to feel very hungry and to think that he would soon have to choose a place in which to come down.

Soon he saw below him a beautiful city, and, best of all, just near the city wall, but outside it and set in a beautiful garden, he saw a palace that seemed to be built of white marble. Coming lower, he saw that this palace had a flat roof, and on this roof the Prince decided to land.

Now though, as was said, he was exceedingly hungry and also rather a rash young man, he now wisely decided that he and the horse had better try to stay hidden on the roof till the sun had set and it was dark. So, on the palace roof and with the magic horse beside him, he sat and waited.

He had, of course, no idea what sort of people might

live in this palace, but he could hear people moving
about below, and soon it seemed to him that he heard
the voices and laughter of girls. As soon as it was dark,
he very cautiously opened a small door. This led, he
found, to a little staircase and, as he hoped, down into
the palace.

Everything seemed quiet, and inside it was very dark
indeed, but at last, at the end of a passage, he saw a
chink of light. Moving softly towards it, he saw that
this faint light came from behind a curtain and, gently
pulling this curtain aside, he found that he was looking
into a large and beautiful room.

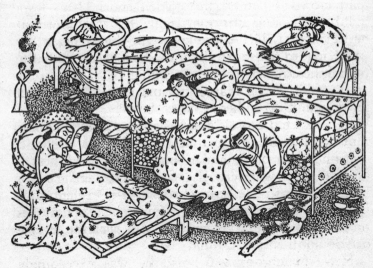

All round this room were divans and cushions, and
on these lay, asleep, a number of beautiful girls. In the
middle of the room, on a couch enriched with gold and
set with pearls, lay the most beautiful of them all, and
on the floor by her side dozed an old woman. The
Prince was astonished by all this, and especially by the

beauty of the girl on the golden couch, for it seemed to him that she was as lovely as a wild tulip. He said to himself that she must certainly be a king's daughter.

Quiet as the Prince tried to be, it was, of course, not long before one of the ladies in the room began to wake up, and when she woke she cried out in terror. Then they all woke and saw that, somehow, a handsome young man had got through the armed guards that always stood at the gate of this beautiful summer palace.

The Princess was the first to recover and soon her old nurse told the others to be quiet.

'For,' whispered the old woman to the ladies, who had crowded behind the golden couch, 'this is no doubt the young Prince of India who seeks to marry our Princess Laila! As you know, she begged her father, the King, to refuse him because she had heard that he was unbearably ugly!'

'But this young man is not ugly at all,' whispered back one of the ladies.

'Of course not!' said the old nurse. 'The King must have sent him here so that Princess Laila could see with her own eyes how handsome he is.'

While they whispered Prince Yusuf had come nearer and had begun to talk most respectfully to the beautiful young Princess, so that any fear she might have had of him should be at an end. He told her as quickly as he could the extraordinary adventure by means of which he had got into her palace.

'If I must go in the morning,' he ended, looking at her mournfully, 'I shall leave my heart behind me, for your beauty has stolen it out of my breast!'

Now the old nurse, still believing that he must be the Indian prince and was there by the King's leave, had already ordered one of the slave girls to bring a tray of sweetmeats and some cups of sherbert. All the girls, and even the charming Princess Laila, laughed when they saw how extraordinarily hungry this handsome young Prince seemed to be, and they all amused themselves by bringing in more and more food. But hungry as he was, Yusuf went on telling the Princess how much he loved her, and soon, though she had begun by being afraid and had gone on by laughing at him, she began to think that she had never seen such a charming young man. All the same, she began to feel only too sure that he was not, as her nurse supposed, the Indian prince, but that the story he had told her when he first came in was nearer the truth.

'I am afraid,' said the Princess at last, 'that when my father hears of all this he will be furious!'

'But will he be angry even when I tell him that I am Yusuf, Prince of Persia?'

'Yes, indeed! I am sure he will. I am ready to believe all you say. I am sure that you really are a prince, and I even believe about how you got here! But the King, my father, will not look at it as I do. You ought—he will say—if you are a real prince, to have come first to him and to have arrived with proper attendants and a letter from your father. Instead, he will say, you came like a thief! If he is half as angry as I fear, he may kill us both. Dear Prince Yusuf, though it breaks my heart to say it, I think you had better go, for he is sure to come in the morning to visit me.'

At that Prince Yusuf declared that he could not bear to leave her, and the end of it was that they secretly agreed that the best thing would be for her to mount the magic horse behind him and for them both to fly back to his father's city.

'My father,' added the young man, 'has only to see you to be sure that you are not only a real princess, but the loveliest maiden in the world! You are like one of the wild tulips that grow on our mountains, you are like one of the roses in our palace gardens. We will make sure that he receives you with all possible honour! I shall go first to him and tell him that you are willing to make me the most fortunate young prince in the world!'

As soon as it began to be light Princess Laila told her old nurse that she just wanted to go for a moment on to the roof to see a beautiful present that the Prince had brought for her, and then off they both ran, up the little staircase. The nurse was old and could only follow slowly, and no sooner were Yusuf and Laila on the roof than he quickly lifted her on to the horse, jumped up in front of her, told her to hold on tightly, and then turned the magic peg. Away they flew, leaving the poor old nurse staring after them and wringing her hands.

Now Prince Yusuf was determined, as he had already declared, to show his lovely princess the greatest possible honour, so that she should never regret having left her father and her own country. To make sure, he unfortunately decided to land with her, not at his father's palace, but at a small summer palace in a garden, rather like the white marble one where he had found her. There he left her with one or two women attendants, kissing her hands and begging her to rest after the journey, and telling her that he would go quickly to his father and tell him what had happened, and that then they would ride out to welcome her royally, and so that she could be brought to her new home with a splendid procession.

Now, while the Prince had been away, the unfortunate King of Persia had been mourning over the disappearance of his dear son Yusuf, while the magician in his turn had been mourning over the disappearance of his magic horse! Unluckily it was the magician, and not the King, who had kept careful watch on the sky and who now saw how the horse had suddenly reappeared again—this time with two riders. The magician saw how it had circled, and had come down, not in the great square of the city, but in the garden of the summer palace.

Quickly running to the gate of this garden, the magician asked the attendants for the news, and, peering round the corner, saw that his magic horse stood at the palace door.

'Great news!' said the attendants. 'The young Prince has come back and brought with him a bride as lovely as a wild tulip. The Prince has just this moment left her here to tell his father and to get his consent to their marriage. The King and the Prince are expected back here within the hour to fetch the bride!'

Then the cunning magician saw a way not only to get back his horse, but also to get his revenge on the Prince. Making some excuse to the attendants, he went to where the Princess was resting. Bowing respectfully before her, he said:

'Lady! Your bridegroom, Prince Yusuf of Persia, has sent me. He begs you to mount the magic horse and to ride to meet him in the great square of the city, where the King waits to honour you.'

Now Princess Laila did not like the look of this hideous old man, and wondered why the Prince had sent such a strange messenger to fetch her. Guessing her thoughts, the magician added in a humble tone, 'Do not wonder, oh most beautiful Princess, that he has sent me! My Prince loves you so much that he could not bear that any handsomer or younger man should come before you, for he knew that your exquisite beauty would instantly have bewitched him! He was also not sure that you know how to control the flying-horse. I am the only other person besides himself who understands it.'

Now it was true that, in their hurry, the Princess had not seen how the horse was made to fly, turn and come down, so, though still with a doubtful mind, she at last consented to go with the wicked old magician.

No sooner had they mounted, and begun to fly, and saw the city under them, than she saw that the King and the Prince were that moment riding out of the palace gates with a splendid retinue and with a splendid litter carried by camels. Seeing this, the horrible old magician flew low, and the unfortunate Prince looked up. When he saw, and guessed what had happened, the Prince's heart grew cold in his breast!

As for the Princess, as soon as she felt that, instead of coming down, the horse had begun to soar into the sky again, she too saw that they had been tricked and began to lament and weep. At that the magician told her roughly to be quiet.

'Henceforth,' he said, 'I am your master! I made this horse and that young Prince took it from me! Now I am revenged, for I have stolen his bride and tortured his heart!'

So, in spite of her tears and pleading, on they flew and at last, when sunset was near, the magician brought the horse down and they landed in a meadow where there were trees and a river.

Now this was in a place far away from Persia, but not far from the city of a certain Greek King. It happened that this king had ridden out to hunt, and, as he was riding home, he saw in the meadow what appeared to be a beautiful black horse. He also saw that, by it, stood a hideous old man in a strange dress, and that before the old man crouched a beautiful young damsel whom he was threatening with a whip. It seemed to him that the damsel was crying out in sorrow. So the King ordered his attendants to bring

this strange pair before him and he saw that the girl was exceedingly lovely.

'Lady, what relation is this old man to you?' asked he. But before she could speak the magician hurriedly answered:

'Sir, she is my wife!'

At that the Princess cried out in indignation and told the King that the old man was not her husband but a liar and a rascal who had carried her off by fraud and force.

Now the King of the Greeks was very ready to believe what she said for, though he was rather old and fat, he had already fallen in love with her. So he immediately had the magician carried off to prison, the beautiful ebony horse—whose magic properties he did not, of course, understand—was put into the king's treasury, while Princess Laila herself was given a fine apartment in his palace.

What was her horror when, next morning, the fat

Greek King came to her and—thinking that she would be delighted—told her that he had just arranged for them to be married the very next day.

'Look out of the window,' said he. 'The whole city is decorated in honour of our wedding!' In vain she protested that she did not want to marry him. He only smiled and nothing that she said would make him believe that she was not delighted with so great an honour.

Meantime the poor young Prince Yusuf, though he determined at once, in spite of his father's opposition, to set out to look for his vanished bride, was in a most unhappy state, for the fact was that he had not the slightest idea where to look! First he went back to her father's kingdom, but there they could tell him nothing, and only mourned the loss of the lovely Laila.

One day, as Yusuf sat in the bazaar in a certain city, and when he had almost given up hope, he heard a group of merchants who were talking about their travels.

'Has the Greek King married his bride yet?' asked one.

'No! How can he? She is as mad as ever!' answered another.

'And what happened to the ebony horse?' asked the first.

'I believe that it is still in his treasury,' answered the second.

As soon as he heard the words 'Ebony Horse', Prince Yusuf left the corner in which he had been sitting and, coming up to the merchants, began courteously to question them, and they soon told him not only about the ugly old man, the beautiful damsel and the ebony horse who had suddenly appeared, but also the name of the Greek city and where it lay.

'Unfortunately,' added they, 'this beautiful damsel seems to have been mad ever since she was found. The

King of the Greeks has called in doctors from every country, but not one can cure her. She is certainly beautiful, but often so violently mad that, if her hands are not tied, she will pull out a man's beard or scratch out his eyes, and she gets no better. By now even the doctors are afraid to go near her.'

Now, not only did the Prince, as he heard this, feel sure that this must be his Laila, but also that Laila was not really mad but had, no doubt, thought of this excellent way of putting off her marriage to the Greek King. He rejoiced greatly, for he now felt sure that she must still love him and must still hope that somehow he would find her, and this thought made him ready to sing for joy.

So, as he journeyed to the Greek city, Prince Yusuf began to think what he would do, and decided to disguise himself as a doctor. Thus disguised, he soon stood before the Greek King and, with a solemn and grave look, bowed before him.

'What is your country?' asked the King. 'And what is your profession?'

'I am, O Magnificent King, a Persian,' answered the Prince, 'and my profession is that of a doctor. Though still young, I have become skilled in my art through deep study. I wander through many countries, curing the sick and the mad. Such, O King, is my occupation.'

'Then,' answered the King, 'you have come to us at the very time of our need,' and he began to tell his story and, though he had heard it already from the merchants, Yusuf pretended to be very much surprised.

'Alas, the lovely creature grows no better, and now it is even dangerous to go near her,' added the King. 'But if, O learned doctor, you can cure her, you shall have as a reward anything that you desire! She is so beautiful that my heart grows weary at the delay in making her my wife!'

Then the sham doctor pretended to ponder deeply and to ask many questions. Especially he asked about the ebony horse and, shaking his head, he soon said that the madness of the damsel was likely to have something to do with it. At last he asked to examine it, for he thought to himself that, if the horse was undamaged, it would be their best means of escape.

So the horse was brought out and, when he had had a good look at it and saw that, luckily, it still seemed as good as ever, the pretended sage said that he must next see the patient.

'I now suspect that her madness is the work of some powerful Jinn who works by means of this ebony horse,' he said gravely. 'It is possible that I may be able to cure her by using the same means, but if she is as violent as this noble King has declared, I must first try to quieten her a little. Your Majesty is welcome, of course, to see what I do, but I must beg that no one

113

should be within hearing, for I must speak secret words of power.'

So the fat King took the pretended doctor to a little lattice window from which they could both see into the Princess' room and she, as soon as she heard footsteps, began to shriek and groan loudly. The King remained at the lattice where he could see, and Yusuf went into her room.

When Laila saw what she took to be yet another doctor coming in, she began to moan and throw herself down, and, in general, so violently did she pretend to be mad that for a moment or two the Prince was unable even to whisper in her ear. But when he whispered her name she knew him! But, looking up at the lattice from behind which the Greek King was watching, the clever girl only uttered a cry louder than before, and then fell down in what seemed to be a fainting fit. The pretended doctor, while every now and

then he loudly called out some word that would sound to the King like a spell, bent over her. 'O delight of my eyes,' he whispered, 'how clever has been your trick!' Then he called out loud, 'Foul Jinn, be silent!' Then he whispered again, 'Now be patient and firm yet a little longer, beloved.' Then he called aloud again: 'Go back among the demons!' and then whispering again, 'If we can only manage things cleverly enough, I have thought of a trick by means of which we can escape from this tyrannical king!'

'I listen, sweet Yusuf!' she whispered back, but then gave a loud groan for the King to hear. 'O treasure of my heart,' she whispered again, 'I will do just as you tell me. OH! AH!' and again she pretended to shriek.

So, like this, they managed to agree on a plan, Yusuf all the while pretending to utter spells and Laila still pretending to cry out. They arranged that, as soon as he left her, Laila was to pretend to be rather better and was to seem weak and quiet, and was to consent to see the King. This was to make him believe in the young doctor's cleverness. Then, after that, the pretended doctor was to announce solemnly to the King that he had now discovered that the terrible madness was certainly caused by a Jinn which worked through the ebony horse and that, for a complete cure, it would be necessary to take both her and the horse back to the original meadow and to let her sit for a while on its back while he performed certain magic rites. There were good hopes, he was to say, that he would in this way be able to get rid of the Jinn altogether.

The Greek King was, of course, delighted when, weak though she seemed, the lovely damsel was able and willing to receive him. She spoke courteously, too, and even smiled, so, after this wonderful proof, he was anxious to do everything that the young doctor suggested.

So next day the King ordered the horse to be carried down to the meadow. He and his bodyguard rode down, too, while Princess Laila, still pretending to be very weak, was carried down in a litter. When she arrived Prince Yusuf, still in his doctor's disguise, was already explaining to the King that it would be necessary to lift the Princess on to the horse, and he begged the King and his bodyguard to stand well back so that, once more, he could see but not hear. He would be obliged, Yusuf went on, to light fires to make a smoke, and to burn magic herbs. He also would, he explained, at a certain moment, have to mount the horse in front of the damsel, when the Jinn might make a fight of it.

'This, O Magnificent King, will very likely make the horse move in a violent way, but do not be alarmed—after that it will all be over!'

The King agreed to everything, for he supposed that what was meant by 'it will all be over' was that she would be cured and he would have his bride again, safe and sound.

So then the pretended doctor lit the fires and made a great smoke all round the horse. Soon he lifted the

Princess on to its back and, after a moment or two more, got up in front of her. Whispering to her to hold on tightly, he immediately turned the pin that made the horse rise, and away they flew, with the Greek King and his bodyguard looking peacefully on! Indeed it was not till he had waited half a day for their return that the fat King, beginning to feel that perhaps he had been tricked, returned sadly to his palace. However, his wise men soon consoled him, found him another bride and assured him that he was well rid of such enchantment and craftiness!

As for the happy Prince Yusuf and his lovely Laila, they flew on all that day rejoicing, and as fast as ever the ebony horse would carry them. At last they arrived at the Persian King's city and, this time, the Prince took care to land just by his father's palace.

And so they were married, amid great rejoicings, and the Princess Laila sent messages to her father

telling him that she was safe and happy, and with the message Prince Yusuf, her husband, sent splendid presents, so that his father-in-law might know that it was in truth to the son of a great king that Princess Laila was now married.

As for Yusuf's own father, the King of the Persians, he decided that he had had quite enough of being astonished, and he had the turning-pin taken out of the ebony horse so that his son should not be tempted into any more dangerous adventures.

So they all lived happily ever after. Prince Yusuf and Princess Laila continued to love each other and, in due time, Yusuf reigned in his father's stead.

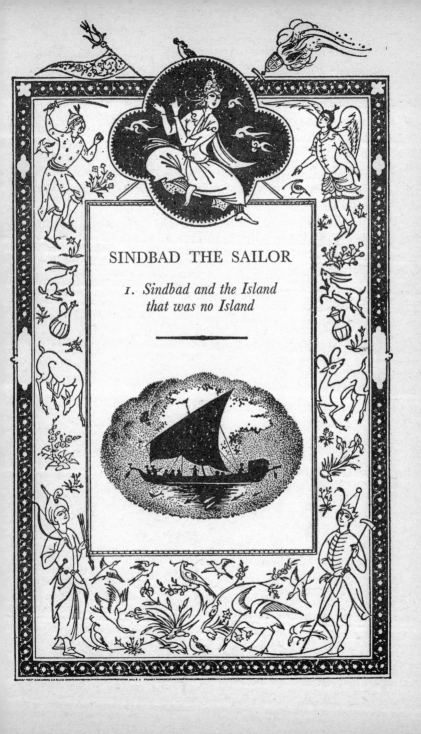

SINDBAD THE SAILOR

*1. Sindbad and the Island
that was no Island*

In the time of Haroun Al Rashid The Glorious, who was for long Caliph and Ruler over the Faithful, there stood in the city of Baghdad a house so fine and delightful that it was almost a palace. There was no dust before it, for here the way was always kept swept and watered. Through an archway that led in from the street could be seen, when the great doors were open, a garden full of shady trees from which came at all times the scent of flowers and the voices of turtle doves, nightingales and babbling water, and with these, at certain times, was mingled the sound of the lute and of voices singing.

Now this house stood on a narrow but busy street. Down this alley, in the burning heat, porters used to pass and repass all day long, carrying heavy loads of merchandise on their heads. Sometimes these porters used to stand resting for a while, looking in at the cool garden, thinking that some people have all the luck, and doubting whether the master, a handsome old man with streaks of silver in his beard, had ever known such toil and hardship as theirs.

On a certain day, when not only were there the sounds of lutes and singing but also the scent of the most delicious dishes from a feast which was going on in the garden, one of these poor porters set down his burden on a bench that stood outside, and leaning sadly in the archway began to make up some verses and murmur them to himself.

> 'Allah made both of us, this man and me,
> Yet I must bear a heavy load
> While he goes free.
> Alas the diff'rence is like vinegar and wine!
> This lucky one has never borne a load like mine
> Or like me known the dust upon the road.'

Hardly had he finished and, turning, with a sigh, had begun to take up his load again, when a handsome little page ran out from the garden and took him by the hand.

'O Porter, lay down your load. My Master calls for you!'

The master of the house and all the guests spoke kindly to the porter and made room for him at the feast. Rose-water was poured over his hands, which he wiped with a snow-white napkin. There were tender little birds wrapped in vine leaves. There were dishes of hot Indian curry, and others of cool dahl; there were sweet peppers stewed in curds. Even the rice was coloured red or green, and there were besides all kinds of sweetmeats and fragrant mint-tea. When he had eaten and drunk the master of the house addressed him in these words:

'O Porter, we heard your lamentation as you stood at the gate, but the thing is not as you suppose, for I too have known hunger, thirst, and toil and also much greater danger. Indeed my experiences have been very strange!'

Then all the guests assured the master of the house that no sound of lute, or fountain, or singing-bird would be sweeter to their ears than the story of his adventures.

 So then Sindbad-of-the-Sea, or, as some call him, Sindbad-the-Sailor—for the master of that house was none other than that celebrated traveller—began to relate his adventures, and they were so many and so strange that one evening was not enough, so that, not once, but many times, all who were at the feast that day met again in the cool garden to

hear him. This was how Sindbad began the story of his adventures.

My father was one of the richest merchants of all the city of Baghdad, but when he died I was still a heedless young man and it was not long before I had frittered away most of my fortune. I did not come to my senses till most of it had been wasted. However, I found that by selling my house and my farm-lands I had still enough money to buy merchandise—such things as bales of cloth and silk, fine carpets, brass-work and the like. With this merchandise I resolved to travel abroad and see if I could not perhaps mend my fortunes by selling it at a profit and at the same time see something of the world and its marvels.

So, one day, I and other merchants embarked on a ship with our goods. We sailed down the river to Basrah and then, putting out to sea, we traded prosperously from island to island and from shore to shore.

At last, after a long sea passage, we came to a small but pleasant island and, since we had been long cooped up on the ship, the captain, deciding to cast anchor, had the landing-planks put out and we all went ashore to stretch our legs. Some of the merchants and the sailors took with them washing-tubs and began to wash their clothes, some began to light fires to cook a meal, and some—of whom I was one—walked about to explore the island.

All at once there were shouts from the ship. 'All aboard!' 'In Allah's name! Quickly!' 'Run for your lives!' 'The Fish! The Fish!' shouted the sailors, and with that they began, in all haste, to heave short the anchor and then to pull in the landing-planks. Then we who were ashore felt that what had seemed to be the ground was shaking under us and I guessed that this was in truth no island but must be a gigantic fish on which, as it lay thus since times of old, sand and earth had gathered, and even trees had grown. But now the immense creature had felt the heat of the fires which we had lit upon its back. Still those who were in the ship shouted, 'Save yourselves! It will plunge to the

bottom! Save yourselves!' So we all ran, leaving everything—food, cooking-pots, washtubs. Some reached the ship in time and some did not, and, in a moment more, the great fish plunged and, with a roar, the sea closed over the place where it had lain.

Alas, I was among those who had not time to reach the ship, and I sank in the sea with those who sank. But, by the mercy of Allah, when I rose to the surface again, I found, floating near me, the largest of the wooden troughs that some of the ship's company had used for washing. I seized it, managed to get astride of it and, tossed and buffeted by the waves, began, as well as I could, to paddle with my feet in the direction of the ship. But alas! In mortal fear lest the great fish should rise again, the captain had already ordered the sails to be hoisted. She was soon far away, I was unseen and my shouts were unheard, and before long her white sails were no more than a speck upon the waters.

When darkness covered the ocean I resigned myself to certain death and with the light of the next morning things seemed no better. But the wind or some current favoured me, and by the end of the next day I was in sight of another island with high cliffs, on which the waves broke and on which I supposed I and my washing-trough would be dashed to pieces. Yet Allah still favoured me, and I managed, more dead than alive, to haul myself out by means of the branches of some tall trees that hung clear of the breakers. It was with my last strength that, drenched and weary, I hauled myself out of the water and then let myself down from the branches to the ground. My legs were not only numb but bleeding from the nibbling of the small fish that had begun to attack me. Darkness was falling, I had no strength to go further, but lay all that night on the ground.

But next morning, when the sun rose, I found that I was not far from a spring of fresh water and from some trees that bore fruit, and, though my legs were still numb, I managed to crawl to them.

I remained thus, very miserable, for several days, but, my strength gradually returning, I began to walk about the island to see if I could find any sign of human inhabitants.

One day, as I thus walked on the shore in a part of the island far from where I had landed, I saw something in the distance that I took for a large wild animal or one of the great beasts of the sea. Walking towards it, I saw that it was no savage or dangerous brute but a beautiful mare, which moved quietly about cropping the grass. She did not see me and I came closer.

Suddenly she caught sight of me and, startled, gave a loud neigh; this startled me in my turn, so that I took to my heels in terror, when, right in my path, I saw a man who seemed to have risen out of the earth.

'Who are you? What are you doing here?' he asked.

'Sir,' I answered, 'I am an unhappy stranger, a shipwrecked voyager, a castaway!'

Then the strange man looked kindly at me, took me by the hand, led me to the cave from which he had appeared so suddenly and gave me food. When I had eaten, my soul became more at ease, and, when he questioned me, I told him all my adventures from first to last. When I had finished I begged him to tell me why he was living in this cave and to whom the beautiful mare belonged.

'I am,' he answered, 'one of the grooms of the great king Mahrajan and from time to time we bring the swiftest and most beautiful of his mares to rest and pasture for a while in this wild and solitary place. We shall soon be returning to the city, when I shall take you to our King and show you our country. Allah be praised that I found you, for otherwise you would have died in misery, none knowing that you were here!'

Upon this I called down blessings upon him, and that night I slept in his cave. Next day I awoke to find that more grooms had assembled from other pastures. They began to collect all the mares and—setting me on

one of the most beautiful—they all mounted and we began our journey to the court of King Mahrajan.

When the King had been informed of how his grooms had found a castaway, he sent for me and, having heard my story, he also praised Allah for the mercy he had shown me, treated me with kindness and honour, and soon made me Comptroller of Shipping at his largest and most prosperous sea-port. Here it was my duty to enquire the names of the captains and the nature of the cargoes of every vessel that put in for trade and to give an account of them to the King. I used, of course, also, for my own sake, to ask the sailors and merchants of every ship if any on board had ever heard of the city of Baghdad or in which direction it lay. But alas! No one knew anything of Baghdad, the City of Peace! None knew of any ship which had ever traded there.

For a long while I continued in favour with the King and with his subjects. I earned the goodwill of the humble because I was always ready to tell the King of their troubles, and of the King and the merchants because I was honest in my dealings.

Indeed for one like me, who had determined to see the world and hear more of its marvels, it was a fine place. One day I would find that the King had in the palace a party of merchants from India, who told me of their country and of the seventy-two races and sects that inhabit it. Another day it would be a party of sailors who told me of strange islands. There was one such not far off, they said, where, all night long, could be heard wild cries and fiendish laughter with a beating of drums and the clash of tambourines.

Many strange things I saw for myself: for example, a fish two hundred cubits long and another with a head like an owl. But, with all this, I began to long for my own city.

One day, when I chanced to feel particularly sad, because there seemed no end to my absence from Baghdad, I happened to be standing on the wharf, leaning on my staff and gazing out to sea. As I looked, I saw a ship which appeared to have a large company of merchants on board and which was making for the harbour with a fair wind. Seeing her come in and that the sails were being furled and that landing-planks were being made ready, I came near, as was my duty as comptroller of the port. I brought out my register and, as the crew landed the merchandise, I began to enter it up. When they seemed to have done I turned to the captain and asked if everything had now been brought ashore.

'Not quite all, my master; I still have some goods in the hold, but the owner of them was drowned during our voyage. Take note of them separately, for I must sell them here and then take back the price to his family.'

'And where did this drowned-one live?' I asked.

'In Baghdad, the City of Peace,' answered the captain.

'What was the merchant's name?' I asked.

'Sindbad,' answered the captain, and when I looked more closely at him I recognized him.

'Do you not know me?' I cried. 'I am Sindbad! By the mercy of Allah I was cast up on this island, where I found favour with the King and became chief clerk of this port. These goods are my only possessions.'

But the captain grew angry at my words.

'Is there no longer faith or honesty in man?' he cried. 'By Allah! Just because you heard me say that

I had goods whose owner was drowned, you are trying this mean trick so as to get them without paying!'

It was long before this honest captain and his sailors, who soon crowded round, would believe that this was no trick but the truth. 'We saw him sink! We saw him sink!' they all kept repeating. But I told them so many things about our former voyage—events from the day we left Basrah till we cast anchor on the island-that-was-no-island— that at last the captain and the others believed me. Then they all rejoiced and embraced me kindly.

'Allah,' they said, 'has granted you a new life!' Then the captain gave me the goods, and I found my name written on them, and so honest had he been that nothing was missing. So then and there I opened the best of my bales and selected a costly gift. The sailors helped me to carry it to the King and I offered it to him as a present, begging his leave to return home. The King was pleased at this end to a strange story and gave me a still larger present in return. The rest of my goods I soon sold at a profit and, with the money, bought the finest products of the island and with much joy re-embarked in my old ship.

Fortune served us, destiny helped us, so at last I found myself once more in my own city—and once more a rich man.

I soon forgot all that I had suffered and, once more, as I had as a youth, spent my time in feasting and pleasure.

To-morrow, if Allah wills, I will tell you of yet stranger adventures.

2. Sindbad and the Valley of Diamonds

After a while I began to feel that I had had enough of this idle life of pleasure.

Instead I began to think of the yet greater pleasures of seeing strange lands, peoples whose ways were new to me, and all the marvels with which Allah has filled the world.

So I shut up my house and, once more, I bought goods for trade. This time I sailed down the Tigris in a small river-boat with my merchandise to Basrah and there chanced to find a fine new sea-going vessel which was about to put to sea. She had new sails, a good crew and a pleasant company of merchants and, on the master agreeing, my goods were immediately stowed in her hold, I myself stepped aboard and we were soon off.

We had a pleasant voyage, calling at this island and that, and at each port at which we landed we met the merchants and grandees, the sellers and the buyers. And so, as we went, we increased our knowledge of the world, our honour and our profit.

At last we sighted a pleasant island, on which, as we sailed nearer, there seemed to be an abundance of fresh water, trees, fruit, flowers and singing-birds, but on which we could see no sign of human inhabitants.

We had been long at sea and, the master anchoring our ship, we all went ashore to get fresh water and to amuse ourselves with the sound of the birds, the sight of the trees and the murmurings of the brooks.

I had taken a little food with me and, having eaten and finding myself by a murmuring stream, I lay down upon the grass and, alas! was soon overcome by sleep. How long I slept I know not, but when I awoke it was to find myself utterly alone. My forgetful shipmates had sailed away without me! Not one of them had remembered me! Racing to the shore, I saw that there was no further hope. The ship was now only a speck on the vast blue of that lonely sea.

Overcome by despair, I threw myself down upon the sand. Once more I was a castaway and utterly alone. I remembered the proverb which says, 'The jar that drops a second time is sure to break!' I blamed myself for my folly not only in going to sleep, but in leaving Baghdad at all. I thought of my wretch plight—for a second time without food or goods, for I had, alas! left everything upon the ship. I imagined, too, that the island might be the haunt of wild beasts or savages; indeed I was soon almost mad with despair.

At last, when I had recovered a little, I climbed up a tree to see if I could see anything more than the loneliness around me. But there seemed to be nothing but sky and sea, sand and trees, rocks and springs of water, and all I could hear was the cry of birds and the murmur of the wind as it gently swayed the branches of the trees.

But at last I thought that I could see, indistinctly through the trees, something different, something smooth and white. But, not being able to tell if it was large and far away, or near and small, I could not even guess what it might be.

Climbing down from my tree, I went cautiously towards this unknown thing and found to my astonishment that what I had seen was an enormous white dome, almost as high as the dome of a mosque but resting on the ground.

I walked round it but could find no door, and it was so smooth that to climb it would clearly have been impossible. I made a mark in the sand at the place where I stood and, walking round the dome once more, found that I had walked fifty paces before I came to my mark again.

Now it was evening, but the sun had not yet set, but, as I stood, the evening light was suddenly darkened as if by a great cloud. I looked up and, to my amazement, saw a great bird hovering above me, and judged that it must be this bird's gigantic wings and enormous body that had darkened the sky.

Then I remembered a story which had long ago been told me by travellers. They said that in certain islands there lived gigantic birds called Rocs—so large that they feed their young on elephants. The dome before me must, I thought, be the egg of a Roc and the shadow above me must be the shadow of a Roc.

And now, as I stood wondering, lo! the giant bird alighted, so that it straddled the dome and, stretching out its legs on either side, seemed to brood over it with its huge wings and body much as a hen will brood over her clutch of eggs. Soon the bird, which had fortunately not seen me, seemed to sleep.

I stood there watching, and as I watched I thought to myself that this bird might perhaps have flown from far. Who knows, I thought, how far this great creature flies by day to find food? It may be that she goes to some other land where there are men and cities. Then, murmuring the name of Allah, who never sleeps, I made my resolve. I unwound my turban, folding and twisting it so that it became like a rope. I bound this rope securely round my waist and then, as gently as I could, tied myself on to one of the great legs of the sleeping bird.

All night long I waited, keeping as still as I could, not daring to sleep, but holding on fast to her leg. At

daybreak (when, as I supposed, she knew that the sun would once more warm it) the Roc rose from her egg, and with a terrible cry and a tremendous clapping of her enormous wings, she rose into the air. Up she soared, higher and higher, till it seemed to me that we must touch the sky. At last, after a long time, I could feel that the direction of our flight was downward, and she alighted. No sooner had she touched ground than I untied my turban from her leg, which was as thick as the beam of a house, for, though she seemed not to have felt my weight or to have known that I was there, I was so much afraid of her that I longed to get away. Indeed, once loose, I trembled so that I had scarcely strength to hide. No sooner was I hidden than I noticed that the great bird was looking this way and that, as smaller birds look for worms. Soon she darted off towards a great, black, long, coiling thing which lay near. Then I saw that this was an enormous, wicked-looking serpent! The Roc now seized the huge creature in her claws and with a great clapping of wings flew away with it.

As soon as she had gone I began to look about me and saw that I was in a desert place and on a steep slope. On one side towered a mountain which seemed as steep as a sea-cliff but very high, while below lay a wide, deep valley. The sun began to burn, there was no water, there were no trees, all seemed desert.

I blamed myself yet again and wished that I had stayed on the island, and I thought with despair how, every time I escaped from one danger, I seemed only to run into a worse.

However, since the mountain seemed unclimbable, I decided to go down into the valley, and what was my amazement when I got there to see that the whole ground seemed to be thick, not with common stones, but with the most splendid diamonds! But this was not all. Unfortunately the enormous and hideous serpent

which the Roc had carried off was, it appeared, only one of thousands; the whole valley seemed to crawl with them as they made off to the caves in which they hid during the day. In a little while, indeed, every small hole seemed to hold a hissing snake, and every cave seemed to hide a serpent so big that it could have swallowed an elephant. 'By Allah!' I said to myself, 'of what use are these diamonds to me? For my destruction is certain!'

All day I wandered without food or drink and watched how certain birds swooped and flew in the hot sky, spying out for any snake or serpent that had not yet hidden itself. These were birds not so great as the Roc, but greater than any eagle or vulture that I had

ever seen, and it seemed to me that they all watched me and only waited for my death. So, most miserably, I spent all that day and, when night fell and the serpents came out once more, I found a cave and, thinking that if any serpent had it for a home, now that night had come it would at least be empty, I took refuge in it. Alas, it was indeed the home of serpents and I soon saw that one of them lay at the back, brooding her eggs. At this my hair stood on end for fear. But I dared not go out and so, the great and hideous serpent not moving, I spent the night there. Once again I dared not sleep, so that, when day dawned, what with sleeplessness, hunger and thirst, I tottered out more dead than alive.

As I walked along the valley where, once more, the splendid diamonds that lay all around shone in the light of the newly risen sun, I came near the steep cliffs of the mountain. Suddenly from these cliffs there fell right in front of me the skinned carcass of half a sheep.

I wondered greatly at the sight, looked round, but could see no one. Then I remembered a story that I had been told long before by a traveller.

This man had told me that certain diamond-merchants who traded in India were in the habit of getting diamonds by a very strange trick. Unable to climb down into the Valley of Diamonds because of the steepness of the cliffs and the danger from the serpents, their trick was to climb the mountains above, slaughter a sheep, skin it, and then, from the cliffs, throw down joints of the meat still moist and fresh, so that some of the diamonds were sure to stick to them. By and by one of the great birds, which have their nests in the mountains, would swoop down on the meat and, taking it up, fly up to their nests with it. Whereupon the merchants would, with cries and a great beating of gongs, sticks, and cooking-pots, scare away the birds. Then, before the birds could fly back, the merchants would quickly pick out the diamonds and leave the meat for the birds as they came back.

No sooner had I remembered this story than I thought of a plan of escape. Quickly filling my pockets and every fold in my clothes with the finest diamonds that I could see, I soon found another and a larger slaughtered beast. Taking off my turban, I once more twisted it into a rope, lay down on my back, shifted the carcase of meat on to my chest, and tied it on firmly with my turban-rope. I had not long to wait before one of these immense vultures, swooping down, grasped the

meat firmly in its claws and, seeming not to notice my weight, flew soaring into the air. Alighting on the top of the great mountain, it was just about to make a meal of the meat when suddenly, from a nearby rock, there was a great shouting, clamour and banging of sticks, whereupon the startled bird flew off.

As quickly as I could I untied my rope and, soaked with blood from the meat, stood up. I know not which was the more frightened, I or the merchant who had thrown down the meat! He now began cautiously to come forward from behind his rock. He knew there was no time to waste, for the vulture would come back. Turning over his meat, he found not a single diamond, so, uttering a loud cry, he beat his breast and looked at me.

'O Heavy Loss! Allah defend us all from the power of the Evil One! Who are you? Why are you here?'

We moved off together and I soothed him as well as I could, telling him I was neither a devil nor a robber and offering him some of my diamonds.

'Accept them, I beg of you, for they are, I am sure, better than those which, but for me, might have been sticking to your meat!'

Soon, hearing voices, other merchants, who had also thrown down meat, came up with us and all were astonished at seeing me there. I told them that I had diamonds enough for them all but was now giddy and almost fainting for hunger, thirst and lack of sleep. So, without more questioning, they took me to their encampment, offered me no violence, but treated me hospitably. When I had eaten, drunk and slept a little I told them my tale; they were so pleased and astonished that they would hardly accept the splendid diamonds which I offered to them, though in truth I had enough to make us all rich.

So, when I had done, we all thanked Allah for his great mercies and they told me that, up to that time, no one had ever set foot in the Valley of Diamonds and come out alive. Then again I slept in their tents for many hours. Next day we all set out and, though we had yet more mountains to cross, and though we saw many serpents and many still stranger sights, yet each night they contrived so well that we always pitched our tents in some safe and convenient place.

So at last, after a long but prosperous journey, we came again to the cities of men and the shores of the sea. I and the other merchants traded our diamonds at great profit, so that, when at last, crossing the sea, we came first to Basrah and then to Baghdad—the City of Peace—I was yet richer than at any former time.

3. Sindbad and The Old-Man-of-the-Sea

When I began again to be weary of the pleasures of the shore and of its idleness, I still had ample money and I decided that this time I would buy a ship of my own, hire a captain and crew to work and navigate her, and let other merchants join me and pay me their passage money. There would like this be no chance, I thought, that I should be left behind on some island. No captain forgets his owner! So, at Basrah, I bought a fine new ship well equipped in every way, with tall masts and new sails.

Once more the beginning of the voyage was prosperous and, as before, I and the other merchants traded from port to port and from island to island and talked with men of many strange lands, hearing marvels and telling our own adventures.

One day we found ourselves near a large, uninhabited island and here I caught sight among the trees of something that I had seen once before—a white dome almost as big as the dome of a mosque but lying on the ground. I, of course, knew at once that this was the egg of a Roc. As the island seemed pleasant, the

passengers begged leave to land. To this the captain and I agreed, but having some business on board, I, unfortunately, did not land with them. As soon as they were ashore they, too, caught sight of the strange white dome. Not knowing what it was—not knowing that at sunset that fearful bird would come back to her egg—they began, just for sport, to throw stones at it and to batter it. It was not long before it broke, so that they saw the young Roc inside—almost ready to hatch. The passengers were delighted and, then and there determining to have a feast, they lit fires, cut up the huge young bird and, coming back to the ship for cooking-pots, called out to me:

'Oh Sir! Come and see what we have found! The dome was a great egg, which we have broken, and inside we have found a young bird almost ready to hatch. We are just about to cook it. Come and join the feast!'

At this I cried out in horror!

'We are all lost!' I cried. And I told them how at sunset, which was then not far off, one or perhaps both of the parent birds would be sure to come back. 'They will be enraged to find what you have done!'

So I called out that we must now push off immediately. Scarcely had they begun to return to the ship when, as before, the sky was darkened and, this time, not one, but two Rocs appeared above us—circling before flying home to their egg.

'All aboard!' I cried, and they, too, were filled with fear. As the captain and crew began in all haste to bring in the landing-planks and weigh the anchor, we saw how the Rocs, flying low, had seen that their egg had been broken and their young one killed. With dreadful screams the great birds wheeled up into the sky. With all speed we set the sails for the open sea. But too late! Once more the sky was darkened and the most fearful cries filled the air and we saw that both birds had begun to chase us and

that each held a great boulder in its claws. The cock bird—the larger of the two—flying directly above us dropped his boulder, but the Captain, by clever steering, managed to make a quick turn which kept us clear, so that the boulder dropped beside us instead of on us. But so heavy was it that the great splash with which it fell almost swamped us. Then the hen bird dropped her boulder, and this one hit our stern so that the rudder flew into twenty pieces and a great hole was torn in the ship's planking, so that she immediately began to sink. Those who had not already been crushed by the boulder sank with her, and of these I was one, so that the dark and bitter waters closed over my head. But, as before, when I came to the surface again Allah was merciful to me. This time it was not a washing-trough, but one of the stout planks of the broken ship that was floating near me.

It was now almost dark and I passed a wretched night clinging as best I could to this plank, but fortunately the sea was calm and, when daylight came, I found that I had drifted in sight of another island. I paddled towards it as well as I could, and crawled up upon an open beach.

After a while, although my fine new ship and all my goods were lost and my captain, crew and fellow-merchants drowned, I began to recover a little and determined to find out what sort of a place it was upon which Allah, in his mercy, had cast me.

I soon found that this was an island as beautiful as Paradise. Its trees bore ripe fruits, its rivers flowed between banks of flowers and the sound of singing-birds mingled with the murmur of many streams. So all that day I wandered about, refreshing myself with the fruits and at night I slept on a grassy bank. But all this while I saw neither man nor any sign of man.

Next morning, though I was still weary and disheartened, I resolved to see more of this land, for it seemed like a lovely garden, except that it was solitary. After a while I came to the bank of a small river, and on the bank I saw sitting a strange-looking old man. He seemed to be either ill or very feeble and to be clothed only in leaves. I though that he might perhaps be another castaway and, seeing his sad looks and guessing that he was not only old but weak, I went up to him and wished him peace in the name of Allah. But he only replied to my greeting by a mournful nod. I began to question him, but soon supposed that he did not understand the language in which I spoke, for, to all I said, he only replied by signs. Presently I began to believe that he had a request and that this was that I should take him up on my shoulders and carry him across the little river.

Now Allah rewards those who do kindnesses, especially to the old and weak, so making signs that I understood him, I bent down and lifted him so that he sat on my shoulders, and was a little surprised to find him heavier than I had imagined. However, I waded across the stream with him. When we reached the other side I bent again, signing to him that he should now get down.

But, instead of slipping to the ground, the old monster wound his legs tightly round my neck. I again made signs as well as I could, thinking that he had not understood. Then I glanced at his legs as they clung more and more tightly round my neck and saw, to my horror, that they were not like the legs of an old man but as rough as the hide of a buffalo. The sight of them frightened me, so now I tried with might and main to throw him off. At this the old wretch only clung the tighter and now began to squeeze my throat so hard with his hands that soon I could no longer breathe, I felt that I was becoming dizzy, the world grew black in front of my eyes, and at last I fell to the ground.

And even now he would not let me be! Loosening his legs a little, he began to beat me over the head and I soon found that he had not only the weight but the strength of a young man. Once more I tried to get rid of him, once more this only made him cling more tightly so that I was almost choked. All this time he never said a word, but only beat me, exactly as a cruel rider might beat a horse. When he got me up again he soon began to force me to go in whatever direction he chose by pointing with his hands and then pressing with his legs.

I found that what he wanted was to make me walk under the trees on which grew the best and ripest fruits. Here the old wretch, sitting at his ease, high on my back, picked and ate as much as he wanted, but scarcely gave me a moment to get some too. If I disobeyed his signs or went too slowly, he would kick and beat me with his arms or his feet and legs so that I could hardly bear the pain.

All that day, weary as I was, I had to carry him and, when darkness came, he made me lie down with him, but the old monster only slept a little and never once loosed his hold, and now and then would kick me up again so that I had to stumble wearily along in the darkness.

'By Allah,' I said to myself, 'is being a slave to this old monster my reward for a good deed? I will never do good to any one again as long as I live!' It seemed to me that nothing that I had hitherto suffered had ever been so detestable as carrying this filthy old wretch!

After many days and nights of this miserable slavery I happened one day to come upon an open grassy place where many pumpkins grew. Some of these were dry, so I took up a large one, cut a hole at the top and cleaned it out. Presently, coming to a place where vines grew, I picked some of the ripe grapes and squeezed their juice into the now empty pumpkin. I then stopped up the hole at the top and put the pumpkin to lie in the sun. Coming that way again after a few days, I found that, just as I had hoped, the grape juice had fermented so that I now had a pumpkinful of strong and excellent wine.

Every day I used to come to this place again and drink a little of the wine, and this helped me to endure the misery of carrying my heavy monster of a master. Sometimes, indeed, when I had drunk a little I would almost forget my misery and my feet would move more quickly, so that he beat me less. The old wretch began, I suppose, to notice that my seeming more nimble and cheerful had had something to do with the pumpkin, for one day he put out his hand as if to take it from me, though I managed to put it out of his reach. Then, a trick coming into my mind, I began to pretend to be drunk and to dance and sing, and what I sang was the praise of wine. All this, of course, made him—as I had intended—want more than ever to taste what must, he thought, have been a magic potion. Next day, though making pretence of trying to keep the pumpkin for myself, I let him have it, and then the greedy old monster, instead of only taking a sip or two, drank all that was left in the pumpkin at one gulp. Now this wine, which had been at the bottom, was the strongest part, and soon he began to sway about on my shoulders and to make a noise as if he, too, were trying to sing. Soon his horrible legs began to go slack and I could feel that they were beginning to loose their hold. Now was my chance. Sitting down quickly, putting my hands under his feet and at the same time giving a violent jerk to my shoulders, I found that I was at last free!

As I saw the hideous creature lying senseless on the ground, bloated and filthy, my heart was filled with hatred for him and his vile ingratitude, and (partly also for fear of what he might do on waking) I took up the first stone I could find, and with it I battered in his wicked skull.

So that was the end of my tormentor! May Allah have no mercy on his soul (if he had one!).

For some days I was happy in my new freedom, for now I could roam as I liked, sleep when I liked, eat and drink of the delicious fruits and excellent water whenever I had a mind to. I had indeed hardly begun to long for human company again when, sitting one day on the shore, I saw a ship which seemed to be making towards the beach on which I was sitting.

Soon she had furled her sails and dropped her anchor, and the passengers and sailors began to come ashore with empty water-casks. When I ran down to meet them, they all gathered round me in surprise at seeing anyone on what they believed to be an uninhabited island and, soon, they were offering me all sorts of kindnesses.

When they heard my tale they told me that it was indeed a marvel that I had escaped.

'Know that the monster who rode on your shoulders was none other than The-Old-Man-of-the-Sea and that you are the first that ever escaped him. Praise be to Allah that you have been the means of destroying such a wretch!'

Giving me food and clothing, they took me with them in their ship and we set sail.

One more adventure I had before I again reached my home in Baghdad—the City of Peace—and if this adventure had not happened I should, this time, have returned a poor man for, as I have told, my goods, as well as my fine new ship, had been lost. But this adventure was the means of profit for me.

I had now no goods with which to trade, and though, no doubt, the excellent captain of the ship which had rescued me would have given me my passage home for nothing, he could not do this, for the ship was outward bound in quite another direction. So they could do no more for me than leave me at their next friendly port. So now, when the ship which had rescued me had left me ashore and had sailed on her way, I found myself wandering about the streets of a strange city trying to find some work in order to gain enough money for a passage home.

As I walked, I fell in with an excellent man who asked me what trade I knew. I told him that, unfortunately, having been a merchant all my life, I knew no skill such as that of tin-smith or leather-worker, or carpenter, or indeed any other trade by which I could now earn money. At that I began to lament, for it seemed to me that it would be hard for me even to live, and still harder to earn enough to be able to return to Baghdad.

When this good stranger saw that I longed for home and was heavy with sadness he thought for a while. Presently he left me, telling me to wait, went to his house and came back with a large strongly made cotton bag, which he gave me.

'Take this bag, O my brother!' said he. 'Go to the beach and half fill it with pebbles. In the morning you will see many men of this city, each with just such a bag of pebbles, and you will see that they go out of the city towards the forest. Go with them and do as they do.'

I wondered at his words, took the bag and thanked him in the name of Allah.

Next morning it was just as he had said. Many men of the city had collected, each with a strong cotton bag half full of pebbles. The man who had given me my bag was there and said to the others:

'This man is a penniless stranger. Consent to take him with you and teach him what he must do, so that he may perhaps gain money enough to reach his home. If he does, those who help him will certainly gain a reward from Allah who—being merciful—loves those who show mercy.' So they agreed and I went with them.

After walking for some time through the forest we came to a wide valley full of tall trees. Now these trees were very high and they had smooth trunks with not a single branch, and at their very top, which swayed in the wind, grew a great head of leaves.

Now we were many and we had not been silent as we went, nor had we crept quietly as hunters do, so that, as we walked, some talking, others singing, the many beasts, such as apes and monkeys, that lived in the forest had been frightened and had swung along in front of us, chattering and jumping from tree to tree.

When we came to the tall trees all these apes and monkeys had climbed up to their tops. Then the men opened their cotton bags and began to pelt the apes with the pebbles. The apes became furious and soon, in their turn, began to pelt us. Then I looked to see what it was that the apes were throwing down. I saw that they were coconuts. So then I made haste and chose a great tree, on which many apes had taken refuge, and I did as the others did, pelting them with the pebbles I had brought, and they did as the other apes had done and pelted me with coconuts. Soon my large cotton bag was full of splendid nuts and, the others having also filled their bags in this way, we all went back to the city well satisfied.

I began to look for the kind stranger who had lent me the bag and who had persuaded the others to let me go with them, and when I found him I thanked him and would have given him all my coconuts. But he courteously refused them, saying that they were all for me and, instead, gave me the key of a little outhouse he had. Here he told me to store the best of my nuts, to sell the rest in the market, and next morning to go out again with the others.

The kindness and goodness of this man—may Allah reward him—was the means of my gaining not only enough money to pay the captain of an excellent ship to take me home, but also to get merchandise in the town where I was, and with this and a fine stock of my best coconuts I was able to set sail.

And so, once more, I was a merchant among merchants, exchanging my coconuts at one island for cinnamon, at another for pepper, at a third for Chinese and Comarin aloes, and at a fourth for pearls. All this I did at a good profit, so that when at last I reached home I was once more a rich man.

4. Sindbad and the Caliph's Command

At last the time came when, counting them up, I found that I had made no less than six of these long and dangerous voyages. In each I had experienced, not only one, but often two or three extraordinary adventures. Once I was almost roasted and eaten for supper by a great black giant as tall as a palm-tree, whose teeth were as long as a boar's tusks, whose ears hung over his shoulders, and whose eyes shone like coals. I had been obliged to see him roast and eat several of my shipmates and had only saved myself by putting out his eyes and then, with much difficulty, had managed to escape his blind hands as he tried to catch me.

Another time I and all my shipmates were made prisoners by black apes, and once, having lived prosperously for some time in a fine city, I had been obliged to go to my own funeral, when having married a wife there who died, by a strange law of that land I was buried alive in a dismal cavern. Once I had managed to escape by making a raft hardly wider than a coffin, on which I had been carried at great speed and in total darkness round the narrow windings of a swift underground stream. When this stream reached daylight again I had seen that I was in worse danger, for it was about to dash with me down a fearful precipice. Fainting with terror, I had only been pulled out, just in time, by the kind hand of a stranger.

Now, in the course of the last of these adventures, I had found myself a castaway on the coast of the rich and beautiful island which is called Ceylon. Here I was taken before the King, who was an excellent ruler and who took pleasure in learning about the world. He listened with pleasure to the stories of all these adventures, showed me favour, and asked me, after I had told him my story, to tell him also about my own city, Baghdad.

I told him that it was a splendid city and that it was ruled over by the most splendid of rulers, the great Caliph who was named Haroun Al Rashid The Magnificent, and whose excellence I praised. After he heard me, the King of Ceylon soon determined to fit out a ship for me in order that he might send, by my hand, a letter and costly presents to his brother ruler, the Caliph. And so, in much honour, having carefully packed away his gifts and letter, I kissed the ground before the King of Ceylon and set sail. I had a prosperous voyage home.

The letter was sealed, but I knew that the presents were magnificent. There were bundles of precious aloewood, a magnificent bed set with jewels such as emeralds and diamonds, and, most beautiful of all, a cup a span high that seemed to be made of a single ruby and whose golden stem was embossed with enormous pearls.

And so, having reached Baghdad, I went before the Caliph, delivered the presents from the King of Ceylon and his letter, kissed the ground before the Caliph, and returned to my own house and, this time, I resolved to adventure no more.

'Allah is merciful,' said I to myself, 'but he may not always deliver me! I am growing past the prime of life and have seen many wonders. What has happened is enough!'

And with that I determined to pass the rest of my life in tranquillity in Baghdad—the City of Peace.

One day, as I was sitting at ease in my garden, there came a knocking at the outer gate. My doorkeeper opened and one of the Caliph's beautiful young pages appeared.

'The Commander of the Faithful has ordered me to fetch you into his presence, O my Master,' said the boy, bowing courteously.

'To hear is to obey,' I answered.

When I had kissed the ground before the Caliph he told his attendants to make a place for me on the steps of the throne, and motioning for a scribe to come near he said:

'Hear, O Sindbad, the letter of the King of Ceylon.'

Now the letter was written on the fairest parchment and the writing was in blue and the whole letter was sweetly scented and dusted with gold.

Then the scribe read:

'Peace be on thee, O Prince and Caliph! This greeting is from the King of Ceylon, before whom stand a thousand elephants and on the battlements of whose palace are a thousand jewels, and who is obeyed by countless princes and warriors.'

'Stop!' said the Caliph to the scribe and, turning to me, he asked, 'Is this true, O Sindbad?'

'It is true, most mighty Prince,' answered I.

Then the Caliph motioned to the scribe to read again.

'We have sent thee some trifling presents. Accept them from a brother and sincere friend. The presents are not suited to thy great dignity, but we beg of thee, O brother! to accept them graciously, and to favour us with a reply and an acceptance of our friendship.'

Then the Caliph motioned away the scribe and began to question me about this King of Ceylon and if what he said about his power, riches, and also his good intentions, was true.

'O my Lord,' I answered, 'this King is truly mighty! Whenever he comes out from his palace a throne is set for him on the back of a gigantic elephant. All his chamberlains and servants carry staffs of gold and the chief of these have, at the top of their staffs, emeralds so big that a man could scarcely grasp one in his hand. This King has a guard of a thousand horsemen who wear silk. His crown is of a splendour surpassing even the crown of Solomon the Great. Also he is a wise ruler. Indeed, he has long ruled his people so well that there is no need of judges in his cities, for the people themselves know truth from lies.'

At last the Caliph said:

'Then it is plain that this letter must have an answer, and also that I must find means to send presents in return to this wise and magnificent king. It it not so, O Sindbad?'

'The Caliph speaks well,' I answered, and with that the Caliph dismissed me.

But he soon sent for me again, and when I had kissed the ground before him he said:

'Sindbad, I have a task for you! Will you do it?'

I answered respectfully:

'What task has the master for his slave?'

'I desire,' said he, 'that you should go to this King of Ceylon with our letter and our presents.'

At that I trembled and said:

'By Allah the Merciful, O my Lord! I wish that you had ordered anything else! For I have taken a hatred to voyaging because of the many troubles, dangers and horrors that I have lived through. Indeed, my Lord, I have even bound myself with an oath never to leave Baghdad again!'

The Caliph was astonished and began to question me. But the time was not then long enough to tell him all my adventures as I have told them here, so that he sent for me again several times. At last, when I had told them the Caliph was still more astonished and said to me:

'The Mercy of Allah is great! Such marvels have never been heard since times of old! I understand your wish! May the word 'travel' never be mentioned in your hearing again! And yet, for my sake, O Sindbad, go out yet once more! Take my letter and presents to this great king and, if Allah wills, you shall return quickly and in honour. For it is not right that we in Baghdad should have this debt of honour and courtesy.'

So I prostrated myself and answered only:

'To hear is to obey!'

So, with a heavy heart, I began to make ready to do as he ordered, and the Caliph sent me the presents and the letter. One of the presents was a magnificent horse with

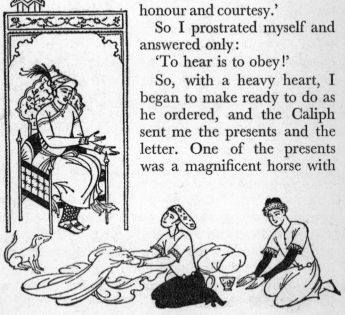

trappings of gold set with jewels. Another was an exquisite book written on the fairest parchment and called *The Delight of the Mind or The Rare Present between Friends*.

There were also silken carpets, the finest white cloth from Egypt and a cup of crystal on which was carved the figure of a lion and of a hunter with his bow drawn. The Caliph also provided me with a fine ship, with her captain, crew, and splendid provisions.

We had a prosperous voyage. When we landed in Ceylon, and when I kissed the ground before the King, he gave me a friendly welcome and presently asked:

'What is the cause of your coming again, O Sindbad?'

So I answered that this time I brought him a letter and presents from my master the Caliph, Commander of the Faithful, and when the slaves had brought in the presents and he had read the letter, the King of Ceylon was greatly pleased. In his delight he dressed me in robes of honour and treated me with the utmost friendliness.

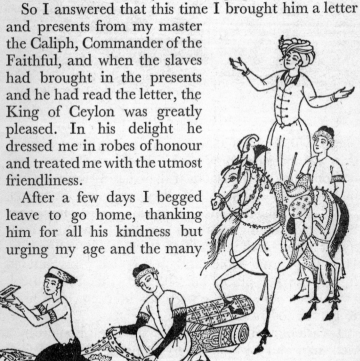

After a few days I begged leave to go home, thanking him for all his kindness but urging my age and the many years that I had spent in travel and my longing to spend the end of my days in my own city. So, though the King pressed me to stay, yet in the end he gave me leave to go. So I set foot once more on board ship and we hoisted sail, and I prayed to Allah that our voyage home might be as swift as our voyage out, for now I had no more desire to trade or to see wonders!

But alas! After sailing for several days with a prosperous wind and that wind continuing, suddenly our ship was surrounded by boats full of armed men—very demons they seemed and, if their hands were not full of bows and arrows, then they were full of spears, swords, or daggers. Those of us who tried to fight they killed and, having captured our ship, they turned her about and took the rest of us to a city they had nearby. Here they at once sold all those who were unwounded in the market place, but, because there was much treasure in our ship, the wretches did not even trouble to get a good price for us.

I was not as unlucky as some, for I was bought by a rich man and he took me to his house, gave me food and drink and, for a day or two, did not set me to any work. At last he sent for me and asked if I had any skill or knew any art or how to make anything.

'O my Lord,' said I, 'I have been all my life, a merchant. I am skilled in nothing else!'

Then he asked me if, at least, I knew how to shoot with a bow and arrow.

'Yes, Lord,' I said. 'That I do know!'

So next day he gave me a good, stout bow and heavy arrows and, mounting on an elephant, set me behind him. We went for some way out of the city and then into a thick forest and at last, where the undergrowth was not so thick, we came to a place of large and tall trees. He told me to take the bow and arrows and to climb up into one of the trees.

'Here,' said he, 'you must remain hidden all night, and in the morning, when a herd of elephants comes to this place, shoot at them with these long, heavy arrows. It is easy to hit but hard to kill, but, if you are

lucky or skilful enough to kill, come back and let me know.' Then he turned his elephant about and left me there.

When the first light of morning came, I could hear the noise of elephants and, not long after, the light increasing, I saw that a herd of these great beasts was now wandering about under the trees. As soon as they were near enough I shot my arrows at them as fast as I could and, with one of my last, was lucky enough to kill one, upon which the rest of the herd immediately made off. As soon as they had gone I slipped down from my tree, went home as fast as I could, and told my master. He was delighted with me, treated me with honour, and sent some of his other slaves to fetch the dead elephant, which was fortunately one with fine tusks. Next evening he told me to try again, and next morning I was again lucky. And so it went on for several days.

But one morning, as I sat in my tree, in the first light of the dawn, I heard that the elephants were coming

much more quickly than before and that there must be many more. At last an enormous herd came plunging into sight, and they now began trumpeting and roaring, with their trunks in the air. Though I stayed perfectly still, it seemed to me that they must have seen me or got wind of me, for some of the largest of them began to form a ring round my tree. No sooner had they done this, than an immense elephant—the greatest I had ever seen—came straight up to my tree, wound his trunk round it and, some of the others helping him, it was not long before they had loosened all its roots. The tree fell and I fell with it. What was my surprise when the great elephant, instead of trampling me to death, as I had expected, pushed aside

the branches in which I was entangled, wound his trunk round me, and set me, quite gently, on his own back. Then, he leading, and the other elephants following, he plunged with me deeper into the forest.

I clung on as best I could, for if I had fallen the other elephants must have trampled on me, and so difficult was it not to be tipped off by his great strides or swept off his back by low branches, that I could hardly tell in which direction we were going. At last, when we seemed to be in a clearing, he tipped me off his back and, in a moment, he and the other elephants were gone!

When my terror and surprise had left me a little, I began to look about me and saw, to my surprise, that,

all around, were the bones and tusks of elephants. Then it seemed to me that the huge elephant must be the wisest as well as the largest of his kind. For he had left me where I could get as much ivory as my master could desire, and that without killing a single elephant!

Now, as I said, this was a huge beast and he had carried me a long way and in such a fashion that I had hardly been able to notice how we came! Because of this it was a day and a night before I was able to find the way back to my master.

When he saw me, he embraced me as if I had been his brother and told me how, when I had not come back at the usual time, he had himself gone to the place, seen the uptorn tree and the marks of many elephants, and had supposed that the beasts must have killed me.

'Tell me, then,' he concluded, 'what was your adventure?'

So I told him my tale and he rejoiced and wondered, and he asked me if I thought I could find that place again. When I said that I thought I could, he at once ordered out his elephant and a strong rope with it, took me up behind him and, without much difficulty, I was able to guide him to the place.

When he saw all the splendid tusks he was greatly delighted at so much ivory, and we gathered up a load, as much as we could tie with the rope, and then set it and ourselves on the back of his elephant and so returned.

As soon as we had stored away the precious ivory, he called me again and, embracing me, told me that I was now free. So I, too, rejoiced and told him of my longing to return to my own city. He answered that he would have kept me with him always in honour, but that he understood my request.

Now the season had come for a fair to which merchants from many countries came to buy ivory. I found among them merchants from Baghdad. So now the man who had been my master paid the captain of their ship for my passage home, and gave me many presents and food for the voyage.

And so at last we came to Baghdad, the City of Peace. And when I had rested a little in my own house I presented myself before the great Caliph Haroun Al Rashid and, having kissed the ground before him, I told him that, by the mercy of Allah, I had been able to obey his commands and taken his letter and his splendid presents in safety to the King of Ceylon.

'And what, O Sindbad,' the Caliph asked, 'happened to you on the way back? For you have been gone far longer than the time to go and to come.'

So I told him all that adventure—first and last.

'Allah be praised for his mercy!' said the Caliph. 'This story is so strange that I shall order my scribes to write it all out in letters of gold.'

And so I took my leave of him, begging him, most respectfully, that he would send me on no more journeys!

Ever since that day I have lived here in peace and so, I hope, I shall live till the end of my days, so that, if the mercy of Allah allow, the pleasures that I now enjoy may make up for the hardships and terrors of all these adventures.

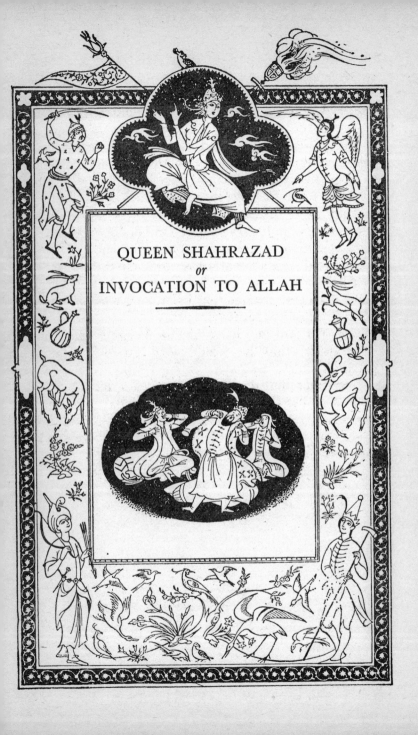

QUEEN SHAHRAZAD
or
INVOCATION TO ALLAH

Thus it was that, (Allah the all-powerful, permitting) Shahrazad, with tale upon tale, not only prolonged her own life, but also saved the King from the wickedness of further fulfilling his terrible vow.

Some say—but Allah knows all—that by her cleverness this telling of stories lasted long. Certain it is that to this day, and in many distant lands, the tales are still often called 'THE THOUSAND AND ONE NIGHTS'. There are so many that there is perhaps no one living who has heard them all.

As to what happened in the end to Shahrazad herself, to the King, to Dunyazad and to the unfortunate old Grand Vizier—all shall certainly be told—but not in this book.

TO MAKE FOOD FOR AN ARABIAN NIGHTS PARTY

This, like the dressing-up (see pages 169-71), is easier than it looks.

It may mean a bit of work, but need not be any more expensive than ordinary party food, in fact, it should be rather cheaper than a party supper because there is less meat.

These are Mohammedan tales, so pork is out. Beef, mutton, and chicken can be used. (Not much meat is usually used for each helping, however, in Arab dishes, as it is rather expensive).

Meat should not be big roasts, but should be small, nicely stewed brown bits, arranged on beds of rice, or sometimes on flat macaroni, together with some kind of stewed vegetable in gravy.

Potatoes weren't brought East from America until a later date than these tales, so they are out for an Arabian Nights feast. Lentils come into accounts of ordinary people's food, so do pumpkins, and of course curry of all sorts. Fish and eggs are often curried as well as meat and poultry, and curry can be made terribly hot or so mild that it just tastes as if a few spices have been added in the cooking. (Yoghurt, plain, is very good served cold with any curry, especially a hot one; a cucumber salad is cooling too.)

Beware of making only a curry for your party: some people, children especially, will avoid any sort.

The rice, or flat macaroni, which should be served as a bed for any sort of meat—then and now—often may be coloured for a feast. Green, red, blue and purple rice look very gay—(the colouring sold by confectioners for decorating cakes is the thing to get.) The grains of rice must be separate of course, not like a rice pudding. Buy a 'long grained' sort. There is now a kind which is particularly easy to manage. This you boil in a special kind of plastic bag, supplied with the rice. But this is slightly more expensive to buy for a large party, and wouldn't be easy to colour.

Other things to serve with meat are cut-up tomatoes, and orange sections (uncooked). The orange is especially good with chicken bits. This is a favourite garnish in Morocco. Stewed prunes, cut in half, a few dates, also cut and cooked, or raisins are other garnishes. No-one, of course, would use all of these with each bit of meat, so think of them as alternatives—as decoration and 'garnishes'.

Cooked puddings are not much eaten, though there is one called something like 'Indian Firmee' which is usually semolina boiled in milk and decorated with little sweets such as 'hundreds and thousands'.

But if there ought to be no ordinary puddings, no jellies or fruit pies, there can be lots of little cakes and sweets. Turkish delight and dates stuffed with almonds are fairly easy to buy at sweet shops. Chocolates are out. 'Kanufa' cake, (which comes into a very nice swindle story 'Maaroof', about a cobbler who becomes a Sultan,) is still made and served. The basis is spiced sweet pastry rolled and cut into strips. The pastry strips are then dipped in honey and rolled up into a flat bun in the way that our Chelsea buns are rolled up— all this before baking. 'Kanufa' cake is not very easy to make and a bit messy but rather nice to eat if you think it worth the trouble. To avoid undue stickiness (from the honey) the completed cake can be rolled in icing sugar, like Turkish Delight.

All kinds of almond-paste cakelets and sweets such as macaroons, marzipan, brightly coloured and moulded into any shapes the maker can manage, are correct. Almond-paste is rather expensive, and also rather solid to eat. Experiment by mixing it with cooked semolina, sweetened and boiled in milk.

'Gazelle Horns' are made out of pastry rolled up. The pastry 'horn' should be a rather long thin cornet and should be stuffed with one of the sweetened almond mixtures.

Drinks

Mohammedans are not supposed to drink wine.

The 'delicious sherbet' cooled with snow that often comes into the tales can be cooled in the 'fridge' or with ice-lollies broken up. It could be made either with sherbet powder from a sweet shop, or, a home-brew made with tinned pineapple juice or any other fruit juice iced and diluted with fizzy or plain lemonade. (True, pineapples were first brought from America by Sir Walter Raleigh, but this is no time to be pedantic.)

For Mint Tea, make China tea in a large pot, but only half-fill up the pot with water. Infuse, then fill up the pot with fresh mint leaves and quite a lot of sugar. On this pour boiling water. Put more fresh mint into each tumbler. No milk. Delicious and most refreshing on a hot day.

Coffee, (if liked) could appropriately be drunk out of the cups belonging to a doll's tea-set. Add sugar in the making as well as in the cup.

DRESSING UP

Dressing up for a fancy dress party can often mean a lot of rather tiresome sewing and—worse—buying expensive material.

But dressing up for an Arabian Nights party or for acting an Arabian Nights play is neither expensive nor difficult if you can borrow such things as curtains and scarves.

Nowadays, in the countries from which the Arabian

A suggested costume for a boy

A simple example of a girl's costume

169

Nights come—that is almost anywhere from Morocco to Persia—a lot of different kinds of dress both for men and women, are still to be seen.

The stories were first written down in the time of our Norman kings, but in Mohammedan countries clothes haven't changed much in all that long time. So, with all that choice it's hard to go wrong or to answer a sensible question such as: 'Ought this lady to wear a veil?'

In Morocco, for instance, a lot of ladies do wear them (always do and always have). But not if they belong to the Berber tribes. It's much the same among Mohammedans in India or Persia. On the whole; the grander the lady, the more likely she is to be veiled.

BOYS

Turbans are wound from a straight length of fairly narrow stuff (say a long scarf) either direct on the head, or, when the wearer already has on a 'tarboush' (high, red, Turkish or Egyptian head dress) or a skull cap, round this so that the top shows. Length of stuff about the wearer's height. For India or Ceylon, secure with gaudy brooches and small plumes to taste.

The loose trousers are really fairly elaborate in cut, but a large square piece of stuff folded with a leg hole left at each corner is fine. To secure the waist a narrow-ish scarf in a contrasting colour makes a 'cummer-bund'. Still more simple is a 'sarong' (Far East) or a 'dhoti' (Indian). The Sarong is a straight bit of stuff, its top selvedge rolled around the wearer's waist in the bath-towel manner and ankle length. The dhoti is a loose, oversize nappie. Both can be patterned and gorgeous in colour. Beards can be 'Father Christmas' beards, dyed say, fox red, or almost blue (fun, but hot).

A white blouse and a bolero jacket (borrowed from a female grown-up because it mustn't have a regular collar) can make the foundation of the upper part, over which cloaks, dressing-gowns and straight or shawl shaped draperies can be arranged.

GIRLS

In Libya and Tunisia, in the street, an all-enveloping bed-sheet, wound round in the manner of the Indian Sari is quite general wear. Under the part drawn over the head, a thin white handkerchief is tied at the back of the head and falls to the breast, so that only mysterious eyes show.

Little girls are not veiled, and, in some Mohammedan tribes (Berbers are one example) grown women do not veil either. For a little girl with short hair, long artificial plaits of black or brown knitting silk, with brilliant tinsel ribbons plaited in can be attached to a jewelled head band under a light coquettish scarf. Necklaces, anklets, bracelets, and earings are all appropriate. Separate small sequins stuck to the forehead, (with small dabs of nail varnish?) should be a feature of a dancing girl's outfit.

FOOTWEAR FOR BOTH SEXES

Footwear would be heelless slippers or sandals. Paint an old pair with gold or aluminium paint and stick on sequins while the paint is wet. Bare feet are a proper alternative. Socks are not permissible.

WHO TOLD THE STORIES? or THE TALE OF QUEEN SHAHRAZAD

To this day tales such as these are told by professional story-tellers in market places of many towns from Morocco to India or Ceylon and beyond—wherever, in fact, Mohammedan people come in from the country to trade.

What you see when story-telling is going on in a market place, is a circle of men and women—mostly men—and if you look over their shoulders you see that there is an inner ring of children who are sitting on the ground.

The story-teller—standing in the middle of this circle—breaks off, just as Queen Shahrazad did, at an exciting place, or when everyone has begun to laugh; he then passes round a bowl and nearly everyone, (except children and beggars,) puts in a copper or so, after which he goes on.

In other parts of the market there may be acrobats or performing monkeys, but as far as I could see in Marakesh (Morocco) in 1971, the story-tellers usually drew the best crowds.

ALI BABA AND THE FORTY THIEVES

Although we think slavery is wrong, there really were a few people who treated their slave-girls well— more, in fact, like adopted daughters.

'Sesame' is the plant whose seeds are eaten and which yield oil which is used for cooking, lighting etc.

PRINCE KAMARELZIMAN AND PRINCESS BUDOOR

Among the really very odd things that happen in this story, there is one that may seem odd, but which can be explained. This is the fact that Budoor and her foster-brother are so fond of each other. How could this happen when she wasn't allowed to see any men? Little Eastern girls (though later they will live in 'purdah' as Budoor did) usually play with any little boys who happen to be about, and, if they share the same nurse, count as 'foster-brother' and 'foster-sister'. The verb 'to foster' shows the meaning.

THE MAGIC HORSE

This is a Persian story and belongs to a time before the Persians became Mohammedans. Persians at that time were known all over the East as magicians and conjurors, and Persian Kings were noted for 'liking to be astonished by marvels'.

The 'Great Feast' in this story would be the Autumn Equinox, a sort of Persian version of 'Harvest Home' or 'Thanksgiving'.

'Yusuf' means 'beautiful' and 'Laila' is the name of the heroine of a famous Persian poem.

SINDBAD

Story-tellers all over the world have passed on stories of mysterious voyages such as these. The tale of the island that turns out to be a great fish also comes into the life of St. Brandon. In this story the monks do exactly what the merchants did, and disturb the great creature by lighting fires on its back. A version of it was printed by Caxton.

The story of the Valley of Diamonds goes back even

further. The raw meat plan was known to the people who went with the famous Greek Emperor, Alexander the Great, to conquer India. There is a further story about this. It is said that on learning that the real danger from the serpents was not so much their 'stings' as that they were so ugly that anyone who saw them died, the Emperor Alexander thought up the idea of killing the creatures by the simple device of providing them with mirrors.

The Caliph in the last story—Haroun Al Rashid— was a real person who ruled in Baghdad in about 800 A.D.

There are a lot more Sindbad tales, but I chose four that I liked best.

Do notice this—in a good many of the Arabian Nights stories people behave rather badly (Maaroof, for example) but the merchants and other people in the Sindbad stories (except of course that horrible 'Old-Man-of-the-Sea' and those pirates) are usually honest and kind.

About the deserted city and all the people having been turned to stone, this could be true in a way. A traveller might easily come back with such a tale, because there really were (and still are) ruined cities that had been gorgeous with statues and stairways decorated with carved bas-reliefs of men and animals, and dating from the days of the Hittites and Assyrians. A Mohammedan traveller in the days of the Arabian Nights might easily think that the statues had once been alive; this would be because Mohammedans are not allowed by their religion to make statues or carvings of animals or plants. Both traveller and story-teller could quite naturally think that if there were statues these had once been real people who had been suddenly turned to stone.

FINAL NOTE ON THE TALE OF
QUEEN SHAHRAZAD

Queen Shahrazad would have known a lot more stories. She no doubt picked out the tales that she thought the King would like; just as I have picked out my own favourites here. It was hard not to put in a lot more, but that would have made the book too long.

But if anyone says:

'What! You don't know the story of the one-eyed Kallenders?' or 'That other story of Sindbad where he gets captured in a cave by a Giant with one eye?' Then you'd better have a look round and you're sure to find them in a book somewhere.

Anyway, you can turn the tables for hardly anyone else is likely to know the story of 'The Half-Lie'.

THE GOD BENEATH THE SEA
by Leon Garfield and Edward Blishen 30p

552 52031 4 Carousel Fiction

This is one of the most important children's books since the war. Winner of the Carnegie Award for children's literature in 1970, and runner-up for the Kate Greenaway Medal, the book is a dramatic, forcefully poetic retelling of the classic Greek myths. It covers the creating of the Gods, the making of man, and the Gods' struggles to control man; into this vast canvas are woven a succession of myths such as the flood, Prometheus, Sysyphus and a multitude of others. This epoch-making book is supported by Charles Keeping's remarkable illustrations.

THE MODEL-RAILWAY MEN
by Ray Pope 25p

552 52024 1

Mark operates his model railway as near to the real thing as possible. Then he encounters the Telford family, miniature people who live only for the railway —Mark's railway. The adventures of Mark and his live passengers will be enjoyed by anyone who has known the delights of a model railway.

PARADE OF HORSES
by Vian Smith 30p

552 54022 6

This is the book for all who love horses. In his affectionate journey through the world of horses, Vian Smith tells of farmhorses and steeplechasers, circus horses, and the breeds which have disappeared over the years such as the fire and funeral pairs. Included are eight pages of photographs, and numerous drawings of different horses.

TRANSWORLD PUBLISHERS. Cash Sales Department, P.O. Box 11, Falmouth Cornwall.

Please send cheque or postal order—no currency, and allow 6p per book to cover the cost of postage and packing.

NAME ....

ADDRESS ....

(SEPT/73) ....